CVC
10

The Winners for Year Ten

Best Story by an Emerging Writer

∽ $10,000 ∽

Layne Coleman

Best Story by a Writer at Any Point of Career

∽ $5,000 ∽

Beth Goobie

CVC

Carter V. Cooper

SHORT FICTION ANTHOLOGY SERIES

BOOK TEN

SELECTED BY AND WITH A PREFACE BY

Joyce Carol Oates

EXILE
editions

singular fiction, poetry, nonfiction, translation, drama, and graphic books

Carter V. Cooper Short Fiction Anthology Series, Book Ten.
Issued in print and electronic formats.

ISSN 2371-3968 (Print)
ISSN 2371-3976 (Online)

ISBN 978-1-55096-989-4 (paperback). ISBN 978-1-55096-990-0 (epub).
ISBN 978-1-55096-991-7 (kindle). ISBN 978-1-55096-992-4 (pdf).

Short stories, Canadian (English). Canadian fiction (English) 21st century.
Series: Carter V. Cooper short fiction anthology series.

We gratefully acknowledge the Canada Council for the Arts, the Government of Canada,
the Ontario Arts Council, and Ontario Creates for their support toward our publishing
activities.

Canadian sales representation: The Canadian Manda Group, 664 Annette Street,
Toronto ON M6S 2C8. mandagroup.com 416 516 0911

North American and international distribution, and U.S. sales:
Independent Publishers Group, 814 North Franklin Street,
Chicago IL 60610. ipgbook.com toll free: 1 800 888 4741

In memory of

Carter V. Cooper

The Winners for Year Ten

Best Story by an Emerging Writer

∽ $10,000 ∽

Layne Coleman

Best Story by a Writer at Any Point of Career

∽ $5,000 ∽

Beth Goobie

CVC
BOOK TEN

PREFACE

In 2011, Gloria Vanderbilt founded the Carter V. Cooper Short Fiction Award, an annual short story competition open to submissions by Canadian writers. Over the years, as more and more good writing was received, Gloria enthusiastically increased the annual prizes to further encourage and support these writers, and as of year three, the winners, in two categories, received $10,000 for the best short story by an emerging writer, and $5,000 for the best short story by a writer at any point in their career.

In 2019, Gloria Vanderbilt died at 95. She had, with eager engagement, always read the finalists, those stories shortlisted by a panel every year, and she had chosen the winners each year. As her good friend, I agreed to take on her role in the year of her death and I chose the winners who eventually appeared in book nine of the annual CVC anthology – although because of Covid-19 it did not appear until 2021, while in that same year a new open-call went out, resulting in this, the tenth and final volume in the series.

And even though the pandemic made administering the competition more challenging, the jurors, though forced apart, worked together with enthusiasm. Then early in 2022 they presented me with their short list – stories that, I have been told by the readers, were surprising and ranged widely in their styles and concerns. Remembering Gloria, I again made my choices.

About the shortlisted stories: it is true, they have surprising range; the writers have told their stories with skill from phrase to phrase, and with a sureness of narrative direction. They are full of the urgent energy writers feel when committing words to paper, no matter their career state or level of accomplishment.

Presenting the year ten winners: Layne Coleman, $10,000 for an Emerging Writer; and Beth Goobie, $5,000 for a Writer At Any Career Point.

I admire the deftness of Beth Goobie's story about a young woman abroad, "One Year." It is truly engrossing. Her ability to imply where the temptation is to clarify makes an awful situation much more dreadful. On the other hand, Layne Coleman's story, "Tony Nappo Ruined My Life," succeeds because he has given his narrator, also a woman, a buoyant, striking voice that does not falter but sustains itself the whole way.

On behalf of Gloria Vanderbilt and the publishers, I want to thank the readers who once again adjudicated the many hundreds of submissions: Randall Perry, Matt Shaw, Janet Somerville, Jerry Tutunjian, F.M. Morrison, and Richard Teleky – each of whom in their own way play very special roles in the development and support of writers, both experienced and emerging.

Joyce Carol Oates

Joyce Carol Oates

Andrea Bishop

AN AMATEUR'S GUIDE TO GOING SOLO

A figure, tiny beneath looming conifers, hesitates beside a weathered wooden sign on the verge of the park boundary. She can likely see her route winding up a short way before it twists across and out of her sight. Behind lies a parking lot, cold, shaded, empty but for one car. White tendrils of moisture rise as the September air warms again after a long cold night.

With tentative steps, she passes by a sign offering guidance and warning of danger: "Allow enough time to return in daylight as darkness quickly hides the trail. Be aware of changing weather conditions. Watch your footing; hazards include dropoffs and cliff edges," but she doesn't stop to read. Maybe she doesn't care. Maybe she's already familiar with the risks. *The first rule of hiking alone is to make sure someone knows your trip plan. The second is to follow it.* Up close, the trail entrance probably appears as a dark hole. Her slender calves are the last part of her that disappears as she ventures in.

✦

One afternoon last April, Katie met her good friend Diane at a pub patio down by False Creek, which wasn't really a creek at all but a long arm of the Pacific Ocean that extended into the city. Diane sat facing the sun, her sunglasses propped on short, bleach-blonde hair, the better to connect with Katie's eyes. Katie had just admitted regret about never having completed a solo overnight hike. She'd meant it as a kind of vague conversation starter, a missed opportunity they both would agree was no longer worth pursuing, but Diane had, possibly intentionally, misinterpreted.

"I love that. Fantastic idea. Let's go together. We'll hike in somewhere together and camp separately for one of the nights. So you get the hang of it," Diane said as they watched Vancouverites shake off the winter blues. Young couples ran along the seawall, respecting white lines that divided running and cycling lanes, pale skin exposed to the sun after a winter concealed beneath oppressive synthetics. On the water, boats chugged out of the harbour under power, halyards clanking, sails wrapped tight against masts. Single and double sculls cut through the lapping waves, the rowers inside rallied by coaches shouting at them through megaphones.

After a chilly morning, the afternoon sun offered warmth. Diane removed her hoodie and seemed comfortable in a tank top, exposing her strong shoulders. Katie, as usual, had misjudged the day and was overdressed in a long-sleeved sweater. Cold beads of condensation grew on her wine glass, gathered momentum, and, at irregular intervals, dropped onto her hand.

Katie tried to backpedal. "Whoa, tiger. I didn't mean right away. I can't get away anytime soon. Besides, it seems so… contrived, I guess, to camp separately. If we ever go, it would be way more fun to stay together the whole time."

"No worries, we both know it's not for everyone," Diane said, chuckling. A long time ago, they'd been on a remote trip to the west coast when, a few days in, and in the middle of nowhere, one of the other women in the group declared that hiking wasn't for her. She simply refused to go on. Diane, their trip leader, had to walk the woman out to where her boyfriend could pick her up, while the rest waited. Katie had joined that expedition with a friend from law school she'd long lost touch with. At the beginning, Katie had thought Diane overbearing, but soon learned it was just a natural efficiency, one of her many competencies. She was also brave and confident. Intrepid. Katie and Diane had been friends that long, almost 25 years.

On the patio Diane's eyes softened. "Katie, you're going to have a lot more time on your hands with Chloe away at school. Enjoy it. Push your boundaries. Live a little."

Katie said nothing. How was she going to cope with the time? Without her daughter? With her husband? Those were the thoughts that kept her up at night.

Diane as if reading Katie's mind said, "You'll be fine, I promise. Just, figure out what you want. Look after yourself for once. Chloe's all good."

"I've spent 18 years making lunches and driving to dance recitals. I'm not sure I even know what I want anymore," Katie said.

"Stop beating yourself up. You've been doing exactly what you wanted all along and you know it. You loved looking after Chloe, and that's okay. That's great, actually. You have raised the most wonderful human. It just might be time to figure out what's next. For you. It doesn't have to be hiking. I get that might not be your thing anymore."

Katie pondered Diane's words. "Do you think, Di, if you make one little change, does it change everything else down the road? Does one change make more, or does everything else stay the same as it always would have?"

"Katie, stop ruminating. Make a change, don't make a change. Hike, don't hike. Just, maybe it's time to… look after yourself. And spend time with your old friends, who've been waiting around for you to have free time again." Katie had the sneaking suspicion if there were such a thing as reincarnation, Diane's soul had been circling the earth a few lifetimes more than hers. They clinked glasses and moved on to safer topics.

-ʌ-

She progresses up the incline. Tree branches form a dense green filter between her and the sky. Moss hangs off the broken and decaying lower branches of trees like shawls folded over phantom limbs. Gnarled roots acting as handholds along the sides of the trail have been smoothed by hikers' hands over years, maybe over centuries. Even the rocks have been worn down by those who've walked here before. Below her pack, the small of the woman's back is damp, darkening her T-shirt. Behind her, the path is packed down, compressed. Moist mounds of leaves rot along the edges of the trail, deep ruddy brown.

The track becomes steep and narrow as it snakes up the rock edge alongside a deep gully, a place the sun never reaches. A sudden gust of wind at the right angle would be all it would take to knock her off the ledge, tumbling her down to the crevice bottom below, where her body, disintegrating, would meld with decaying foliage and the bony remnants of animals who'd previously misstepped.

A young man, bare-chested and energetic, passes her on his way up. She climbs onto the tiny perch above the cliff to make room for him to pass. Keeps her head down. Doesn't talk. *Ascending hikers have the right of way; if you're coming down, move off the trail.* Nobody is coming down the trail yet, it's too early in the day.

—⁊⁙⁊—

Katie had been relieved when Chloe finally picked a university that was only a ferry-ride away, but still worried about her impending departure. She'd prepared herself as best she could, had probed her other mom friends casually over the preceding years. "How's Julia doing away at school? Was she able to make it home for reading week?"

One evening Katie couldn't help herself, though she'd tried to raise the subject before and been shot down. "Just curious if you think you'll get together with your Vancouver friends here on weekends or stay on the island."

"Geez, Mom, would you drop it?" Chloe had said.

"Oh, leave her alone. How could she possibly know?" Mike said from the other room.

He often stepped in as referee. If they'd had a boy, would their roles have been reversed? Was he also worried about how the two of them would adjust to their extra time together? She would have liked to ask him his own plans for coping, but vague questions frequently irritated Mike, and she was unlikely to get a useful answer anyway.

"Mom, I love you. I'll see you lots, okay? Don't worry so much." Katie got a quick hug from Chloe.

Katie wondered if Chloe was more open with Diane these days. When Chloe was a toddler, she'd been hospitalized with meningitis. None of the grandparents lived nearby and they'd been grateful when Diane had stepped up to help them out, even postponing a long-awaited canoe trip up north. Diane kept the two of them fed, the house organized, and Katie from breaking apart under the double threats of fear and loneliness. Diane met her husband, Adrian, at Chloe's hospital, but it was a while before Katie could joke around with her about something good coming out of that dark time. Chloe was too young to remember her illness, and Mike and Katie rarely mentioned it, but a special bond remained between Chloe and Diane. Still, Katie had learned the hard way not to inquire too much about what went on between them.

⌐⁄\⌐

She crests the trees, steps off the trail, and, settling on a smooth rock platform, removes her pack to search inside. Water in the stream running parallel to the trail tumbles over rocks above her with a burble, mist dancing in the air and catching in the light. Sword ferns grow among the rocks, sucking nutrients from the river and soil. The water carries on deep into the crevice below, shimmering beckoningly, deceivingly, in the distance. Massive dragonflies, their forms little evolved over hundreds of millions of years, weave about, approach her face and hover before pivoting away. One lone horsefly circles with increasing speed above her head.

She looks up at the giant round boulders lining the edges of the deep river valley and shudders. The minivan-sized rocks had tumbled down from above during the previous spring thaw, when snow and ice had melted and frozen and melted again until with a pronounced roar, the powerful river had overflowed its banks, carrying trees and boulders and life down with it to the river valley bottom below. *No matter how long your hike, as a precaution, be prepared with enough food and gear to stay out a night or two longer than you intended. Otherwise, do not bring anything you don't absolutely need.* When the shadow of a cloud passes over the rock she's been sitting on, the woman shivers and quickly packs up her few belongings.

─╱╲─

Late the previous evening, when Katie found herself home alone and felt the cooling September breeze, she decided it was time. She knew if she didn't go soon, she never would. It wasn't the solo overnight that she and Diane had planned, but a day hike on the nearby Stawamus Chief was at least a step in the right direction. Walking had always been a comfort, the rhythmic movement of her body lulling her mind until it stilled.

After an unbearable summer, Chloe had departed as planned for her first semester at university. Mike was away at a conference where he'd been long booked to give the keynote speech but left only at her insistence, saying he'd pop back in a heartbeat if she needed him.

Katie stood in the basement deciding what to pick from the bins of old camping gear. The Chief would only be a day hike, so she wouldn't need much, but as Diane always said, you still need to be prepared. *Even for a day hike, you need the 10 essentials. And, always, appropriate footwear.* Should she take a first aid kit? She weighed it in her hand, put it in the small pile. If she brought too much the heavy pack would slow her down, but she didn't want to leave anything behind she might need in an emergency.

Each piece of equipment was accompanied by a memory. Here was the blue and yellow tent Diane had passed on to the family after the first and final camping trip Adrian agreed to take with her right after the two had met. The tent had been roomy enough for Chloe to cuddle in between Mike and Katie on their various car-camping excursions. There were the two matching sleeping bags she and Mike used to zip together before Chloe was born. And there was the red hiking pack she'd bought for that first Juan de Fuca trip with Diane. On that expedition, way back, before they'd even swapped names, Diane had dumped out Katie's pack, removed at least five pounds of what she considered to be excess food and equipment, and walked abruptly away. Later, Katie had appreciated the reduced load but lamented losing the stash of chocolate she'd originally hidden deep inside.

While Katie packed, she thought about her last visit with Diane. Diane had been preparing for a nine-day solo traverse of the Stein Valley. The first and final parts of the trail were well-maintained, used frequently by weekenders who hiked out and back over two to three days, but Diane had set her sights on traversing the whole route including a long piece in the middle which was not well travelled.

As usual, Diane was confident but packed carefully. It was a considerable undertaking, even for her. She stood in front of the set of shelves mulling out loud over what gear to take. "The down one'll be warmer but I could be in for a week of rain." She picked out a green, mid-warmth, synthetic sleeping bag and laid it on the bench. "Did I tell you about the kittens we rescued from the storm sewer last week?" Katie tried to keep up with Diane's thoughts and movements. When Diane selected a set of nested metal pots from the next shelf over, Katie trailed after her. "Done. What's next?" Diane asked. Katie had a copy of Diane's checklist in her pocket and ticked items off for her.

The conversation swung around again to getting Katie "back out there."

"You could still come with me and do your solo overnight, you know," Diane said. "You can have the tent, and I'll sleep under a tarp in the woods. Sometimes I do that anyway. I really wouldn't mind."

"Come on, Di, there's no way I could pull it off. Nine days?"

"We can shorten it. Do the out and back we originally planned. I'm only doing the whole route because you bailed on me," Diane said, but she was smiling.

"I'm sorry, Diane. I'll come soon, I really will. Just not quite yet. Chloe leaves in a month for her job away at summer camp and then she's off to university. It could be her last month at home ever."

Diane raised an eyebrow.

"Seriously, Diane, I don't want to waste any time I could spend with her. Not waste. I don't mean it like that. You know what I mean. You and I can go hiking anytime."

"She'll be home all of two minutes the whole time we're gone, and you know it. Mike won't mind. He'd probably enjoy the time alone with her. I'm going anyway, so there's no pressure. In fact, I'd love the company. It couldn't be more perfect," Diane offered.

"I can't. I'm sorry. I need more time to prepare. Next year. I promise."

"All right, love. I'll drop it. But you're welcome to come if you change your mind."

And back to the discussion of which tent Diane should take to best accommodate this in-between season, her summer tent which weighed less or the four-season one that was sturdier. Like always, Diane threw a few tips Katie's way. *Pack light and then take something out. Waterproof everything, even if you're sure it's not going to rain.* Most of the advice Katie could already recite, but it was comforting to hear Diane remind her.

She arrives at the top of the mountain. The terrain has flattened into knolls of gently rounded rock. Crooked and stumpy evergreens, cousins to the tall trees at the base of the mountain, cling determinedly to the rock in minuscule patches of dirt. The resources here are limited. No moss. No ferns. Few places for animals to shelter. Her footsteps raise a cloud of dust from the chalky trail roasting high up in the September sun and her shirt is wet, discoloured ovals soaking beneath her armpits.

She scans the plateau, targeting a location with eyes first, then with legs that seem to resist forward movement until she comes to a standstill on the highest piece of land. After looking up at the sky, searching, she drops onto the smooth, sloping rock beside a tiny pine. The light is fading. The other hikers have come and gone. She collapses onto the ground with her arms pressed hard into the earth as if attempting to soak up the last warmth lingering in the rock. She doesn't last long. She collects her daypack and heads back to the trail. But she slows again, stills again. Turns around and returns.

Gangly trees throw increasingly large and shaky shadows her way as the lowering sun speeds along its trajectory. A creature scurries up behind her, then scrambles away. Before she turns around, it has already retreated into the shadows. She'll never know what it was or where it's gone.

―⁄ι∖―

As it turned out, when Adrian called Katie two weeks later the timing of her visit with Diane proved to be useful.

"Katie, Diane isn't back from her trip. She's two days overdue. You haven't heard from her, have you?" he asked.

Katie, processing, mumbled in the negative.

"Didn't think so, but I needed to be sure. The ranger checked, and her car's still parked at the trailhead where she started. I've got a helicopter lined up to check it out. If I don't hear anything by morning, I'm sending him in to see what's going on."

Katie started to speak, but Adrian cut her off.

"It looks like the small green solo tent is missing. The ultra-light summer one. Is that the one she took?" he asked.

"Yes," Katie confirmed.

"Do you remember which coat she packed?" he asked.

"She has her black raingear. Navy puffy."

"So help me, God, if I pay this guy and she walks out of the woods and tells me she felt like she just wanted an extra day, I might kill her this time," Adrian said.

It wasn't just Adrian. Nobody was really worried. Not at first. It was so Diane to linger an extra night or two. Diane, at her least cooperative and most independent. Diane, who was so experienced, so capable, and, sometimes, so self-indulgent. At the time, Katie had been helping Chloe submit applications for university scholarships and was irritated that her niggling concern reduced her concentration.

Adrian called again early the next morning. "Katie, they flew over and saw nothing." Adrenaline spiked down her arms. Black spots appeared in her vision. She could feel the beat of her pulse in the crooks of her elbows. One, or even two days, over-due on the trail wasn't too worrisome. Any number of minor hassles could have delayed Diane's arrival by a day or two. But she should have been easy to spot from the air. Katie knew danger was binary in the backcountry. Everything was fine until it wasn't.

"No sign of her. I'm going to drive up there," Adrian said.

"I'll come, too," Katie said.

"Uh, no. No, maybe you should stay here. Would you? Someone needs to be around if she calls. There isn't great service up there, and I know she'll call you if she can't get me. Don't you think?" He sounded panicked, unsure, like he was hoping anyone else would handle it. Katie realized that Adrian probably also felt intimidated under the strength of Diane's competence.

Katie agreed to stay back. Was Diane lost? No way. Not Diane. Not possible. Was she hurt? Maybe. She was probably sitting in her tent with a broken ankle, under her sleeping bag with an emergency blanket on top, eating a small snack and re-reading her one book with the cover and extra pages removed, waiting until help arrived. That was plausible. *If something goes wrong, ration your food and spread it out. You don't need to eat much at any one time, and you don't know how long you'll be there.*

A few hours later, Adrian texted he'd arrived. The helicopter was coming back to get him, and they'd do another flyover. Search and rescue had been notified. The Royal Canadian Mounted Police, too. The RCMP. Jesus. First phase. Locate the subject. Katie lowered her head.

Later that afternoon, a man from Search and Rescue called to interview her.

"How well did Diane know the area?" he asked.

"I don't know. Okay, I guess. Actually, the part in the middle? Not well. But she'd make herself familiar with it. Ask Adrian, he'd know," she said.

"Of course, but we'd like to know what you think."

"Oh. Well, no, she didn't know the whole route well." Did Katie think she was an experienced hiker? Yes, very. Extremely experienced, in fact. How were she and Adrian getting along? Were they fighting? No, not ever. If she'd gotten lost, how would she react? Lost? Diane? She wouldn't get lost. She was competent in the backcountry. How was her mood when she left? Was she feeling down? What? No! How much extra food did Katie think Diane took with her? Very little, probably. Extreme rations for two extra days. That was her rule. Ten per cent. Enough for the two days that were already gone.

The next day, Katie texted Adrian. Heard nothing back. Called his cell. Held her breath during the rings. She knew the service up there was terrible; it wasn't Adrian's fault, but still she swore at him when it connected to voicemail. At 4:10 in the afternoon, there was no phone call. No call at 11 after. Or 12 after.

Adrian did phone a few hours later but said there was no sign of Diane yet. Nothing. No tent, no campsite.

"I wish I had better news," Adrian said.

Katie tried to swallow but her throat was too painful. She said, "You'll find her. It's okay. You'll find her soon."

"Not tonight. They're done for the day. They won't go. Not after dusk when they don't know where to look. They need to locate her first."

"I'm coming up."

"It won't help. They won't even let me go out on the search anymore. There are tons of volunteers. Lots of locals who know the area. They're mobilizing again at first light."

For most of the next day, Katie waited for news. She sat and stared into space. She walked aimlessly around the house and tried not to let Chloe see how upset she was. Mike worked from home to keep her company, but listening to him get worked up over trivial office politics just made things worse somehow. Finally, Adrian called.

"They found her campsite."

"Oh, thank God. Is she okay?" Silence. "Is she okay?"

"They didn't find her, just her tent and some of her stuff. But her daypack is missing, her tarp, a few other things, so we think she has those. Wherever she is. They're doing a ground search now. But Katie—" he choked and paused. "Katie, they have a large area to search. Her last campsite was only about four days in, and it doesn't look like she's been there for quite a while."

After they hung up she made assurances to herself. "They'll find her. Relax. They'll find her soon." She whispered entreaties to the planet. "Look after her. Please look after her until we can find her." Whispered promises to Diane. "We will find you. I know you must be scared. Sit tight a little longer and we'll get you out of there soon."

That night when Katie lay down she saw Diane bent over a camp stove, efficiently preparing a meal. She shook the memory away. Opened her eyes. Tried again. Saw Diane laughing, a full-face crinkly to the corners of her eyes laugh. Katie sat up. Her phone had only moved ahead one minute.

The following day Adrian informed her that if search and rescue didn't find anything more by the end of the day, they were calling off their critical response team. At least 10 days had passed since Diane slept in her tent. There'd been two late spring snowstorms in the meantime. The team felt the probability of survival was too low. Of course, volunteers in the area would continue to remain vigilant, but search and rescue said they needed to pull back, citing "limited resources."

The next day Adrian sent the final text. "I'm sorry. They're done." And just like that, Diane was officially declared dead. The search team laid out the possible scenarios and probability of each. Most likely Diane had left her planned route for a spontaneous day hike, slept under her tarp, woken to a blanket of snow, lost the trail back, and become disoriented. It doesn't take long to become hypothermic and most of Diane's warm clothes were at the tent. But there was no real explanation. Diane and her daypack were just gone.

Adrian came home. He was a wreck. Chloe cancelled her summer job. Mike took time off work and rarely checked in. One day ran into the next and Katie struggled with the most basic of tasks. Chloe stepped up to help, but Katie struggled with that too, even telling her harshly one day to back off, before apologizing in tears. There was a service, and Katie was surprised to meet friends and relatives of Diane's she'd never heard mentioned. Still, Diane didn't feel dead to Katie. Just missing, away on another trip.

—⁊ᴵᶜ—

At the top of the mountain, she collects twigs and branches from the ground and places them neatly in a rock depression. She fumbles while digging matches out of her safety kit, spilling a few on the ground, then pulls an old paper out of her coat pocket and studies it before shoving it under the pile of wood. She sets it alight and returns to her seat.

With the sun already dipping behind the neighbouring mountains, the forest below tips from deep green into dark grey. Darkness ascends, but a clear mauve sky dances with colour and vitality above her head for a bit, until the foreground changes colour from grey to black, and the shapes of the sur-rounding mountains change as well. Low hills in the distance transform, growing in size and proximity with the increasing darkness until they are no longer distinguishable, but instead, merge into one substantial bumpy tableau. *Enjoy it. Push your boundaries. Live a little.* She shouts at the sky, and there's only the faintest echo of her voice off the distant mountain range in response. Shaking, but with one firm hand against the rock, she weeps.

After pulling herself together, Katie focuses on building up the fire. She adds twigs to keep the flame bright and larger sticks to sustain it.

The fire makes a jumpy little flame, and though Katie feels like she might be engulfed by the surrounding darkness, she sits firm. She wishes she could tell Diane she's doing this. She pulls her puffy coat out of her pack and spreads it across her lap, tucking the edges tightly under her legs. She tugs a headlamp out of the emergency kit, tests it, and places it in the pocket of her sweatshirt, within reach for when the impending darkness becomes too much. After a while, she pulls out the last of her food, a dark chocolate bar she'd stuffed in the bottom of her pack.

The fire cracks loudly and Katie startles, swinging her light in an arc, but all she can see is rock and dirt and the vague shape of trees in the distance. She's alone.

Of course, there is not one moment when dusk tips completely into darkness, but after a bit, Katie knows she's committed to the long dark night ahead. And while it doesn't subside, she eventually gets used to the thumping of her heart. She finds it both unfamiliar and disconcerting but not entirely unpleasant.

Later, to her gratitude, a round moon rises, and grows bright enough that she can see her surroundings more clearly. She sits, the minutes stacking up, waiting for dawn, where, from her elevated vantage point, she'll be able to see the sun rise.

Her spot is close to the edge of the giant rock. Close enough that when she stands to add to the fire, she can see all the way down to the earth below but not so close that she might fall over the edge. Someone had walked over the precipice a few years before, whether lulled into it by the pull of nature or by accident nobody knew for sure. Although she can understand the appeal of it, Katie knows she never would. And neither would Diane. Her thoughts eddy and swirl. She obsesses on the terrifying what-ifs of Diane's last minutes, despite knowing those moments were only a tiny portion of the total time she'd had on earth.

James MacSwain

THE TEAZER

The Mahone Bay Gazette, June 27, 1813

The main Lunenburg wharf was crowded yesterday with news that the *Teazer*, a Yankee privateer, was being chased into the harbour by a vessel of our British Navy. It was a cunning trap but the *Teazer* seized on a NW wind and tacked between Cross Island and East Point, knowing that the shoals would prevent the big-bottom British ship, the *Orpheus*, from venturing after her into Mahone Bay. A local captain, Ab Mosher, and volunteers slipped our coastal schooner, *La Hague*, which had recently been outfitted with a one-pounder, and raced to catch and board the *Teazer*. Trapped now in Mahone Bay the *Teazer* strained to escape. Suddenly there was a terrific explosion as the *Teazer* disintegrated into a flaming fireball. A squall of rain and fog enveloped the scene as *La Hague* searched for survivors. Out of a crew of 65 only seven were saved, several with grievous injuries. This reporter was privileged to interview a young American sailor with only a broken arm. His testimony that Lieutenant Ariel Johnson, who had been paroled in a previous encounter with the British and had sworn never to go to sea again as a privateer against Britain, panicked and threw a flaming brand into the magazine. If captured, he would have been hanged and hung in a gibbet on George's Island as a traitor to the British Crown. The fear so seized him, spake the young Yankee lad, that he sacrificed his comrades to the terrible blast of several kegs of lethal gun powder.

The Monologue of Lieutenant Ariel Johnson

Freedom! Perhaps it's an illusion. Muskets firing into flesh of my flesh; once dead, the dead tell no tales or that they lived at all. Mother always said I was the pessimist. Professor Daniel berated my lack of empathy while I said I was hard-nosed like all my ancestors and proud of it. Lust knocked the ground from under me. I cherish it now and what an energizer it was, skimming lightly over all those bothersome domesticities and do this and do that. Then it was the flag flying and freedom!

I've kept a diary since I was 16 and Amelia, my cousin, tried to grab it when I sat writing in the window seat under the stained-glass window of climbing red roses. I wrote that the light in her eyes was a deep black sparkle and I realized she was playing the flirt with conviction. The flush of youth can be a wanton wager. I read Wordsworth and Coleridge and tried to be romantic and then…and then…I kissed Arnold the gardener. And he kissed me back.

Once the restless sea has ravished you with its endless horizon and the promise of transcendence, then you are ready for the hard work. There are numerous ropes to learn, sails to furl, and then on a moment's notice haul them into the trickster wind. Not to mention cannon and cut-throats and pistols at ready. All the pretty men are consumed by their destinies. Even the enemy can be handsome.

My parents are negative about my going to sea. They have no idea that I've escaped into a world that encourages comradery and holding your rum while staring into the fog on watch for two hours listening for the snap of enemy sails or the crash of waves on a rocky shore. In the lee of the wind my lover's warm arm steadies me; he brings me my grog. My comrades don't judge even if they disapprove; survival in the teeth of the storm trumps all morality.

The Monologue of the Map

Cross Island. Blue Rocks. The Ovens. Rose Bay. Mader Cove. Bluff Point. Refuse Island. Big Tancook Island. East Ironbound Island. Little Duck Island. I admire them all; not that they admire me, these hardscrabble rocks that'll drown you as soon as look at you. With their spruce and brambles, home to thousands of birds all squawking and pooping and out there on the rim of the ocean where there be frights and daring waves. I'll stay here, just linen paper and ink, and watch the schooners sail away, thank you very much.

These fisherfolk are a hardscrabble lot themselves; Bluenoses who laugh at fear although they take a gander at me and their eyes cross as they trace with a finger the coves where they hunker down out of the wind. Oh, they're all for education as long as it don't interfere with the angels dancing on the head of a pin. Or how canny they know the winds; some of them just know the weather deep in their bones. I shiver and roll up, just put me away safe and sound. Sometimes I just have to roll myself up and leave my master gaping in displeasure.

There's always storms here. And the winter! The winter is a sorry time, all cold with a cold that will peel your skin loose and swallow you in a fit of fury. I remember when I arrived here with Sir Crane, my master the magistrate, on a blustery day in August, never knowing that a few months later we be trapped by our fire while a three-day blizzard hammered at the door. Then Sir Crane unrolled me on his cold desk and I yelped at him. I couldn't stop myself. Although I was that sorry after; ice floes in the harbour were my undoing.

Of course, when spring arrives the winter is forgotten. The summer heat can be terrific when it's still and the humidity lingers. The roses burst forth in all that dew, especially where the cemetery meets the sea; on Sundays it's a favourite stroll and you can see far out to where my islands glimmer on the horizon. You can see where all my contours switch and curl and clamber down to the water and the tumble of white foam. You can see my master skimming over to Big Tancook and a booze-up with the boys.

The Monologue of the Witch of Mader's Cove

I'm a Mader; we Maders, some of us anyways, have a snarl inside our heads. It comes upon us, the women, in foreshadows of death and stormy disasters that rear up against all reason. The vision shudders and groans in my mind; I remember hanging clothes on the line, the wind warm and comforting, then black and cold and looking out at a squall of rain and lightning coming down, the very one that had frightened my dream the night before. I was all of seven and rushed to my mother who calmed me with soothing words that now and then the ancestors throw as a warning to the living.

Now I'm the old witch with my brewing pot of fog; the very one who conjures the flaming ship to appear to iron-hearted fishermen or innocent boys on a spree, both. They say my eyes leak mist, my hands spill lightning bolts and my nether parts shoot out vapours to seduce exhausted sailors. When I hear such tales I laugh and snicker and clap my hands; to be feared is good news for one such as me, a lone woman with 70 years hanging on me.

The flaming ship, the *Teazer*! I've gotten a lot of mileage out of that one, a whispered word to the women who come to me on the evening tide; I tell them another pot of brewed trouble has flared and the flaming ship with burning sails haunts the Islands and all atwitter they rush away to gossip about my shivery visions. The truth is they come to me for my potent herbs, both to abort and to relieve the pain of birth. Life and death, that's my actual witchery, and it must be veiled with tales of ghost ships and supernatural sightings of the undead.

Men are such skittish creatures when it comes to superstitions, worse than the women. I've had men with the evil eye hanging from their necks hidden under their woollies. Along with Saint Christopher nestled in their fur. I've heard the tales of the *Teazer*, how Ariel Johnson threw the brand into the magazine. That is not true; it was his lover, Abednego McCrae, him with the tattoo of the fairy Ariel between belly button and balls. They supposed their first names would protect them. But the flames took them.

The Monologue of the Storm

Truthfully, I am only a fiction. Most of the time I'm written up in the newspaper or these days you turn on the radio or the late-night news; winging down the electrical wires rides the disaster, the catastrophe of the storm, the terrible storm with ocean surge and wind that knocks not only your socks off but every stitch you own. Death is evoked and everyone shivers. Don't tell me you don't like a good storm as long as you're safe and sound under the covers and your precious life continues with its usual exuberance.

Now and then you are the centre of my vengeance. I've grown strong on the flesh of the drowned, the sailors with their grog and their biscuit and their potatoes. They keep trim but oh how delicious! And none of them can swim. Why bother; when I devour them their agony is quick. The cold waves shriek for my pleasure. Come dine, they shriek, and I roar back my ecstasy and shred another sail. When your roof flies off and the covers go careening into the wreck, I pluck you from your nest and swallow you whole.

Sometimes I am not so ravenous. The blizzard smothers the house. The snow is cold, but you are warm with the iron stove and plenty of wood. How I love to listen to your fireside chatter; I sigh with you over dead ancestors and the young boy off to war. The drifts of winter, the gusts of spring, the thunderstorms of summer, the hurricanes of autumn pass through and repeat in your tales; leaning in to lower your voice so the ghosts don't hear some salacious detail that muddled their lives. I listen intently to every scandal.

One whose eyes are moist whispers how grandfather and Uncle George, whose hair turned white the night he saw the burning ship out there past Mader's Cove and the fog turning red from the flames. I remember I inhaled my wispy breeze and exhaled a bank of mist and rain to shadow my feasting. How the little ones quiver; the flaming ship burns again and again to disturb their fears. Fear the storm, I shriek! Then I moan and rattle the windows. Truthfully, I am only a fiction.

The Second Monologue of Lieutenant Ariel Johnson

Betrayal is the knife that pierces my heart and enrages me; I slash and burn the petty merchants and their cargos as the betrayal simmers and scorches my bones. I am at my worst; I try and curb my thought of them in each other's arms, their coupling behind the barrows of rum and salted kippers. I know I'm obsessed, their flash of heat while all the waiting squeezes our stress to the point of boredom and restlessness, when sailors get restless the captain slings the grog to all and sundry. I get very drunk.

Then the waiting splutters into action. Sails on the horizon are spotted, the bell clangs, all hands on deck, the chase begins, we pour on the sails and the speed. A shout, we all turn to the east and see the armed vessel of the British line bearing down on us. We turn and run and slice the waves cursing the trap. The captain stamps up and down. Their cannons roar with plumes of smoke and they gain, they chase us into Lunenburg Harbour. We scrape by Ovens Point, reckless in our panic.

Abednego McCrae saunters up to me and I push him away. He slips and slides across the deck and swears, gets up and comes at me with his fists. I retreat as the *Teazer* swings about to escape into Mahone Bay and I too fall and slide into the scuppers as the sea washes over us. McCrae is bloated with hate as he pummels my face. The First Mate separates us and orders us to desist and face the enemy. We shoot into Mahone Bay and I fall again, blood pouring from my broken nose.

Now I am truly doomed; if we survive, Captain MacDonald will have me disciplined and if we are captured the English will snap my neck. I stagger down to the galley and punch out the cook. I seize a great wooden spoon and thrust it into the banked stove where it bursts into flame. It flares brightly, scorching my hand, but I grasp it tight, careening down the corridor from side to side I reach the magazine and fling the spoon into the midst of the gunpowder kegs and fall back and pass out.

The Second Monologue of the Map

Kings Bay. LaHave River. Hell Rachets. Pearl Island. Gooseberry Island. Oak Island. Gaff Point. Cherry Cove. Heckman Island. Hartling Bay. It's all of a piece, rock that's been torn apart and rammed back together all threaded with seams of granite and scrubby dirt that spits out a few vegetables. Lackland it is and there's only the fishing that's tangible since there's plenty of wood to build the schooners but then there's also plenty of storms to smash them to smithereens.

My master has succumbed to drink. Half the time he leaves me unrolled and several times has spilled rum on my precious, expensive elevations; men from the Royal Engineers don't come cheap with their calibrations measuring the contours of our wee bit of earth. This rocky coast swirls about the sun; even the little ones know that we swing around Ol' Sol and that the seasons march one after the other because of it. Their grandfathers laugh and nod wisely because they're relieved they didn't perish in the cold Atlantic.

Everyone drinks heavily here and I wonder that anyone survives the fisticuffs that potent spirits induce in all and sundry. I curl up, traumatized, sensitized, cringing away from the terrible paws of my master stabbing at me with his dirty fingernail. His gold wedding ring glimmers in the lantern's light and I have to snort; then he drools or worse, throws up his fish and potatoes. I snap at him. A little paper cut on his throat sobers him somewhat.

Now he's inscribing with a pen an "x" wherever the fire ship has been spotted. Gouging into my uniform blue ocean and bays and inlets and coves he seeks to rationalize the moon's waxing and waning with the swirls of fog and drizzle. He spins theories of the thinness between this world and the world of the dead. I deny that ghosts haunt my headlands and harbours while he rips open wounds with his steel nib thus effecting their eruption among us.

The Second Monologue of the Witch of Mader's Cove

There's nothing like a pot of tea with a dash of rum and brown sugar from the Barbados. A good stir and you're ready for the morning weather, which now is seemingly disrupted by headwinds from the north. It's always on top of you just when you think another storm has blown itself out. Of course, they blame me and my witch's cauldron, which always has nothing more damning than a soup of moose meat and turnips and carrots bubbling away.

I do see a death now and then; it seizes me; the feeling is wretched and I wail and moan, the pins and needles in my muscles, especially in my arms and legs, goes on for hours. I find myself lying on my floor with some anxious woman leaning over me. I clear my throat of silt and phlegm; it was the ghost of Ariel Johnson, I say, with his flaming hair and his jealous eyes all wicked with agony. She helps me to my rocking chair and dishes out the tea brewing on the hearth.

Of course, it's all lies. It's just me and the explosions in my head; the doctor calls them strokes, spasms in the old veins exhausted by all that pumping. The only forerunner they announce is my own death. Although when Sir Crane, the magistrate, the drunken old fool, fell through the ice on East Ironbound I was visited by a vision of him and his bottle disappearing beneath the ice cakes. The air got all freezing around me; when I awoke I staggered as close to the stove as I could wrapped in my quilted eiderdown, the one I embroidered with astronomical symbols to support my supposed witchery.

I was called by my bladder the other night and cursing I slogged my way through a summer rain to the outhouse. Some they say have put in the new-fangled indoor toilet; perhaps I can scare them into putting in one for me, how my old bones would love that. I heard a cry that stopped me in my tracks, the rain drumming on my head, and there coming through the apple trees a flaming ghost of a man. I keeled over; when I woke I was drenched and had peed myself from fright. I got a laugh out of that one.

The Second Monologue of the Storm

I scrape everything down to the bone, clean the nostalgia from your eyes, revel in the hysteria of your petty loves and hatreds, render your political feuds of greed and corruption as so much dross and vaporous bluster. Lord of all you survey? I throw all that to the four corners; I seize your flesh, and I'm blowing it away. The ruins of high-rises are in my sights.

After the storm your insurance is shot. Your dams are broken, the floods sweep away the cattle, the dogs, the farmland, the cars. The electricity sparks and shuts down, the meat turns rancid, the roads are gouged and shattered. I retreat to the upper atmosphere and applaud the suicides, the mental anguish, and I exalt. Nerves are shattered. I plot to promote your extinction.

All the creatures of destruction are on the loose. I have seized the fireship, and it is mine. I send its flaming ruin careening along your coasts, saturating your habitations with smoke and fire, choking lungs and searing hair. The drowned dissolve into torrential rains, my ghosts shake the earth with their curses, my demons ride the wind and snap trees into kindling.

Why don't you surrender and go quietly? The lords of the sea, the sky, and the land have divorced you. Your failure to conserve the earth is the death of you. Go! I'll still be here, roaring away and tearing clumps of continents into grains of sand, filling the seas with melting ice, searing deserts into existence. You will experience the fate of the fireship; perhaps your auras will linger for a while, then vanish into legend.

Kate Cayley

NEIGHBOURS

We, the parents, had two fears. Of course, we had more than two, but at the moment these were the two I thought about most. One we discussed freely, standing in our little groups that broke and reformed through some kind of instinctive pattern, which from the outside would have looked as arbitrary as what gathers together or drives apart a flock of small birds. Even with the ostensible egalitarianism of our lives, these sudden clumps (in the schoolyard, in the park, in front of the grocery store) were mostly women, men absent or standing in their own huddles, having their own conversations, which seemed to me to maintain a lighter tone. I don't think this was because the fathers were in better moods or less frightened of real or imagined threats. They were just more guarded.

The first fear was the man. He lived with his mother at the end of my street. I didn't know his name, and it seemed to me that no one I knew did, from divisions of class and differences of language which had hardened into habit over time. I assumed he was Portuguese, like most of the older families who had already lived on the street for decades when I bought my house. He was probably 45, with the drooping nose and chin of a Roman emperor, brown hair swirling around a bald crown, the skin raw pink in the cold fall air. He walked through the neighbourhood, his blue windbreaker open over a white T-shirt, loose jeans, work boots though he didn't seem to work; in fact, his boots were weirdly pristine, as though they had just come out of the box. He talked to himself, a small grumbling like a dreaming dog. I hadn't thought much about him in the 15 years we'd lived in our house. My daughter and son walked themselves to school every morning and often passed him on the corner, on his endless strolls. He never, as far as I knew, acknowledged them. He was simply part of the back-drop of their childhood, like the half-blind old lady who fed pigeons, calling them into her yard. Then there was the alley-way, and we couldn't think of the man and our children with-out thinking of danger.

The second fear, which we didn't really talk about, was the woman. That was only a rumour. She would have to move somewhere, but no one knew for sure that she had moved here. She was believed to have changed her name, dyed her hair. She was married; she'd found someone willing to marry her. She was older, of course. I'd seen a murky photograph of her com-ing out of a house that could have been a house near where I lived. She had two children now, like me. In the picture, she wore huge sunglasses, a dark coat swinging to her feet, her attempted anonymity itself conspicuous.

We didn't dwell on what she'd done. We'd been younger then, most of us just leaving our own childhoods, our parents turn-ing over the newspapers when we came into the room.

I'm being fanciful when I say we shared this second fear. The woman wasn't often mentioned; I only assumed that everyone else thought of her as I did, as often as I did. There had been a flurry of attention recently: a cover story in a magazine, a few online petitions. She must have been present in my neighbours' minds, an apprehension if not a fear. It wasn't a fear for me, either, not exactly, it was more a worry, in the way I might worry at a torn cuticle, gnaw at it absently until I tasted blood.

I thought I'd seen her once. Walking ahead of me as it got dark. I only rarely used to go out at night; now that my kids were not always with me it had become more common. I made myself leave the house at dusk, hoping to feel more at home in the fading light, anxious that I was becoming fastidious and lonely, locking my door early and watching social-issue dramas in bed, spending too much time online and becoming righteously angry about the opinions of people I'd never met. So I walked, often until it was fully dark. She moved quickly, swathed in a grey poncho. She stopped at the crosswalk and turned to press the signal button. The light caught her. We looked at each other briefly before she looked away and crossed. I felt my mouth open, wondering what I would do if she looked back again, feeling there was nothing I could do except stare, no expression I could summon that would be enough. Afterwards, I was ashamed of myself, performing for an unseen audience, and remembered how disapproving I'd been when I'd read that some of the nurses at the hospital where she'd given birth had refused to touch her.

But thinking of her under the street light, the heavily made-up prettiness of her small, pointed face, it made sense to me that the nurses would refuse to approach that unthinkable body. Not even from horror, though that would be part of it, but out of superstitious bafflement. How was it possible she existed?

I had recently separated from my husband. This is not supposed to matter, but I felt it, a subtle shift in the schoolyard tone, the glances you might give an unhappy child, believing they do not notice. I was not alone: women who were also divorced or queer wore the same smiles I did, practised and accommodating, while the other women talked about their husbands with aristocratic disparagement. We nodded at the idiocies of husbands. We tried not to feel left out.

I work from home as a copy editor, my income augmented by support payments, so I felt I needed the time in the schoolyard more than most of the others, but some people (even people who I thought were in the same boat) were unsure about me. I had been very clumsy in the immediate aftermath of the separation in a way I couldn't repair, not without addressing how I'd behaved directly, which would just call more attention to it. I'd talked loudly about my husband, unable to stop even when I knew I should, even when my children or their friends were in earshot, even when I was talking to someone who knew my husband as well as they knew me, or better. I'd painted my nails dark blue and bought a pair of lime-green, spike-heeled boots and I'd laughed in a snorting, guttural way, half-noticing that the sympathy I was offered was made more ardent by being embarrassed, yet not able to stop myself, like someone just sober enough to know they are humiliating themselves but too drunk to care.

Anyway, alone at home, I thought about the woman under the street light and risked hoping that we would run into each other again, that we would talk, with me not letting on I knew who she was. We would go out for coffee, I would study her across the table, trying to hide my fascination, but she wouldn't notice, she would be someone who fed off fascination and took it as her due.

I was so alarmed by this daydream that I tried never to have it again. I believed in forgiveness, in absolution and second chances, but only tenuously, an inherited article of faith that I hadn't tested. I didn't know what I would say to a monster if I actually met one.

It was Cynthia who'd seen the man in the alleyway. She arrived at school before the bell rang, hurrying across the grass and gravel, looking for someone to tell. She found us. Yes, she was sure, she knew what she'd seen. If anyone doubted her they could go look and find the coil of human shit. She'd been coming back from the Sobey's, taking the shortcut to her house and there he was, squatting in the alley in front of a garage door, pants at his ankles. He was holding a roll of toilet paper for when he was finished. Looking away from her, I imagined, with the strained and urgent expression I remembered from when my children were still in diapers. Of course, she'd kept walking, breaking into a run as she neared the street.

I was standing with Mai and Lauren and Shannon, listening to Cynthia describe him, her voice a little shaky: the alleyway, mid-afternoon sun, the unreal moment of eye contact, not knowing whether or not he meant himself to be seen. The strange exhibitionism of it, less expected than a flasher or a public masturbator, the queasy question of what would happen to the evidence he'd left on the concrete. Shannon listened, half-smiling.

"Maybe he just really needed to take a shit," she said. There was a pause; nobody could tell if she was making a joke, and I wanted to be her friend.

Shannon lived with her husband and three children on the other side of the bridge; our daughters were in the same class, not exactly friends but familiar with each other. I'd been to her house a few times for birthday parties. Her husband, whose name I could never remember, ran some kind of small construction company; their house was always under renovation, with exposed lathe or a gap somewhere in the floor or ceiling, but was understood to be on the way to perfect completion. She served margaritas to the parents at the birthday parties, wore purple lipstick and set out massive bowls of gummy bears and chips, letting the kids sink their hands in, and she giggled at the orange dust and red jellied streaks left along her walls. Her husband admired her, I thought, as he watched her hand out plastic cups of Sprite, seconds of cake. He looked at her defencelessly and I thought no one had ever looked at me like that. I didn't want her husband but they seemed to fit together in a way I thought I had never fit with anyone, with myself. So I was fairly deep in my self-indulgent sadness, as though I was a younger woman, a young woman, a girl, 13 or 14 years old, with sadness my only source of authority. And when she smiled and dismissed the man I wanted to be friends with her in a way that made me think of childhood, that intensity of want that is as overwhelming as anything yet encountered, prior to sex.

"Isn't he harmless?" Shannon asked, but she said it as a challenge, and didn't expect to be answered.

No one answered her. But by the next morning, he wasn't. Someone knew his cousin, someone knew about a restraining order against him from his cousin's ex-wife, knew about his mother cowering in her room. I eyed the house: shut blinds, brown siding, lawn ornaments arranged on the weedy square out front. Squat gnomes, deer with blobby pink noses, the casting's seam ridging their backs, faded to dirty white. A motorcycle was sometimes parked beside the ornaments when the older brother visited. He wore a red bandana, exuded a greater menace, with his rasping voice, hands studded with blackened silver rings. When I saw them together on the steps the younger brother quailed, shrunken in his failure to be free of whatever past they shared.

I warned my children about the man. We stood in the kitchen, avoiding the formality of the couch, of serious talks, which they were leery of, at nine and 11 just old enough to despise the textbook pieties that my husband and I had used to tell them we were separating, not yet old enough to see that we were falling back on those phrases because we were at a loss. I was overwhelmed with relief at having phrases to say and I meant them. *We love you. This has nothing to do with you. This is not your fault.*

When I turned 40, my husband and my children made me dinner and a cake with a ring of white candles. My daughter bore the cake toward me and it listed slightly to one side. They cheered when I blew out the candles, and I was unambiguously and unexpectedly happy. I did not wish for anything else. I did not wish to be anywhere else. The smoke from the blown candles curled into my eyes and my son turned the lights back on and I sank the knife into the cake and was happy. Only six months later, when we sat the kids on the couch and told them nothing was their fault I wished for another set of words that would have reminded them, me, to remember that that moment with the cake was as true as this unsurprising conversation. That would have persuaded us that we had been capable of happiness, and even sometimes known what it was when it arrived instead of only recognizing it in retrospect.

I had not been very good at noticing happiness, though I realize this is not an uncommon problem. I can't make up my mind whether this is a sign that I, and many of the people I know, are irredeemably spoiled, made tremulous and petty by the peculiar, slightly sterile abundance of our lives, or whether this is just human, to find the quotidian unbearable as it is lived, even while knowing that, after a disaster, we would long helplessly for every mundane detail, curse ourselves for taking anything for granted. I was aware of how much I'd taken for granted, but it made me fixate on other, bigger disasters, as if I would now be punished forever, my luck run out. My marriage over, I saw omens everywhere, like a biblical literalist looking for signs in the weather.

Warning my children about the man, I emphasized that he was probably fine, but that we would make a list of common-sense rules. If they saw him, then cross the street. If they were walking alone when they saw him, they were to come home. Avoid his house, where he would often be found, standing on the porch, surveying the street. Avoid the alleyway. That was already a rule, but one I knew they broke.

"What if he speaks to us?" my daughter asked.

"He never speaks to us," my son said, shrugging.

"Then don't answer," I said.

That night, I dreamed about the woman. It was completely innocuous, not even worth interpreting. We were walking side by side, hesitatingly sociable, pushing strollers. The thing was, in the dream, I didn't think about what she'd done and I'm not even sure I was aware of it. She was just another person I sort of knew, like the women I talked with in the schoolyard.

When I woke up, it was already 5:00, so I got out of bed. Made coffee, planned school lunches.

I don't think I was dreaming about her because of some deep desire for violence. I don't think I had one. I think I am more or less decent and I think the people around me are, as well, more or less. Most people are, or at least try to be, or want to be thought to be trying to be. I very much want to be thought to be trying to be decent. And some kind of fixation, some conviction that people are vicious creatures, seems to me as sentimental as the opposite conviction that we are good. I don't think I am good. Just hoping to be decent, or at least not exposed as whatever it is I am. The uneasiness of those little groups was the unease of wanting to be seen to be good. I saw that look on other people's faces, mostly other women's faces, but I felt it most strongly on my own, as we twittered together like birds.

I wanted to be friends with Shannon because I suspected she didn't care about being good, or being thought to be good, or anything to do with goodness, one way or the other.

It turned out to be easy. I was walking down under the bridge, thinking about the woman, thinking, underneath that, about my husband and the way he cried on the night he left, so abjectly that I pitied him, as though he'd erased his announcement three months before at our marriage counsellor's office that he saw no way forward. He'd said that, *no way forward*, in a way that made me think of his job – government PR – in which he must often have to say trite things that carry an air of irrefutability, but are in fact made more irrefutable by being meaningless. Though this had a single, blunt meaning: *I do not love you. I do not love you anymore.* He'd said it so evenly, with ironclad calm, and then got up, put on his coat, left the door open behind him, left the counsellor and I staring at each other.

The night my husband left, I stood on the porch smoking. The kids were at his sister's house with their cousins so we could have privacy, which seemed unnecessary under the circumstances, but I was glad they were gone as I watched him sob and gasp his way along the sidewalk, to disappear at the corner. I smoked three cigarettes in a row, throwing them into the early-spring snow. I am not a regular smoker, and never more than one at a time, so they made me nauseous and light-headed, which felt like sorrow or freedom, or both.

As I went into the house I saw a figure standing under the street light and for a moment I thought he'd come back. Then I thought I'd conjured him up, my subconscious supplying what I wanted, that no one was there at all, and that made me wish I had more cigarettes. I couldn't bear how much I hoped for him to come back.

Now I think it was the man, pausing on a midnight walk, the blue windbreaker zipped up to his throat but still just the T-shirt underneath. He'd stopped, wondering at the retreating sound of my husband weeping.

When I heard footsteps behind me I sped up, since I was under the bridge and the bridge made me jumpy even though it was early afternoon. I heard my name called. It was Shannon, in a long, blue wool coat. She gave a little skip and caught up to me.

"Where are you going?"

"Just to run a couple of errands."

She squinted at her phone.

"Come have coffee with me instead. You've got hours till pick up."

I attempted the little hesitation that would show I wasn't desperate, but she lived on the second street after the bridge, and steered me into her house, walking ahead into the kitchen. I took off my coat, hung it up, smoothing down the folds in an attempt to make it stay on the overfull rack. It fell twice, and I left it in a heap over my boots.

I remembered the kitchen as plates piled in the sink, pizza boxes teetering on the granite counter, wads of paper towel stained with pink spills, the shrilling of over-sugared bouncing children almost visible, like the sharp spots from the pot lights. Now the lights were off, the room illuminated by the two sky-lights above, which gave the cleanliness a sombre, cathedral feel. Canisters lined the free-standing counter, dark stone flecked with silver and white, which bisected the room. Everything I could see ceramic, glass, moulded wood, the slapdash plastic-wrap element of child-raising trotted out only for parties. The long dining-room table shone dark, on the other side of the room by the sliding doors. She filled the espresso pot.

"The cleaner just came," she said over her shoulder. "Sorry. It was a present from my parents for my birthday last month. So you can't see any of our crap."

She waved at the cupboards.

"It's all still there."

She turned to me, leaning against the counter, one hand tapping lightly on the other, and it was nice, feeling that her kitchen made her self-conscious, that she wanted to impress me, that she liked me.

"Well, it looks beautiful," I said, wondering what else I could say. I went over to an open magazine on the table, though

Shannon made a slight movement of wanting to hide it. One of those respectable glossy magazines that still aren't above true crime as long as it contains some sociological analysis. *Where Is She Now?* the headline read, alongside a collage of photographs of the woman: the central blurred image of her coming out of a house (the same picture I'd seen, the house that could have been on any of the streets around mine), and surrounding it, the other, familiar pictures. Her arrival at the courthouse. Her husband. Her wedding, blonde hair teased, eyes lined cerulean, the skirt frothing out in tiers of white lace, the bodice sewn with pearly sequins. I turned the page. More photographs of her, smaller this time, boxed among the text. There were no photographs of the victims, which might have been out of respect for the families, except one, the outline of a head in a security video, bending toward the woman, who was leaning out of a car, smiling up. I think it was used in the trial.

Shannon brought over two cups, a jug of milk, sugar.

"I know it's gross, but I got obsessed," she said.

"I think I saw her," I said, though I hadn't meant to say it, or not in the way I did, like she was a visiting star.

Shannon sat down. We talked. We compared stories we'd read, theories we had. It was the most intimate I had been with anyone for a while. She told me her husband hated it so much that she had stopped bringing up the woman, that she deleted her search history, suspecting he might check. I told her about my dream, about pushing our strollers together, going to the grocery store. Telling the dream to someone felt amazing and humiliating, like playing a confessional game at a party and finding you've confessed too much, like describing a sexual fantasy to your partner and being answered with a fraught smile and silence. I laughed while I told it, but I told it, and she nodded slowly, offered herself as a teenage girl, lying awake imagining she would rescue them, crash through a window and rescue them, and this story became so satisfying, so detailed, that it lulled her to sleep. She was mortified by it now, of course, which was why she wanted to tell me. I could see why it would help a young girl sleep. I liked the matter-of-fact way she told it. Determined to make us even. We drank more coffee and ate an entire package of cookies and ran out the door late for pick up. When we got to the school she stopped me at the gate and whispered into my ear.

"What?" I said.

"I want us to find out where she lives," she said. "I think we can figure it out."

My son stood glowering by the wall. My daughter, who didn't need to be fetched anymore, was already hidden by a swarm of brilliantly dressed girls, gripping phones, shrieking to be heard over one another. Shannon's husband was there.

"Isn't it my turn?" he asked, and she kissed his cheek.

"Thank you. I forgot," she said and stepped back to where I was, sad again, reminded that I was alone. But she took my arm.

"We finished the cookies," she said, "and we lost track of time," and I was folded in, her arm tight through mine.

We saw each other often in the next few weeks, one of those playground acquaintanceships that abruptly leap toward friendship, going for coffee after drop off, texting each other jokes, unkind comments about teachers, the school principal, even other parents. We made up nicknames. Sometimes one of us would text from across the schoolyard while we talked to other people.

Did he bring up Hitchhiker's Guide to the Galaxy *yet?*

Don't let that Parent Council snack Fascist get on your good side. Remember she got chocolate milk banned.

Do you think she makes that face during sex?

Don't be too hard on the principal. She doesn't have any friends.

Rescue me. She's about to tell me about her allergies.

She didn't work, so she texted more often than I did. I tried to keep up. I lost time composing, erasing, rewording, and then more time fretting as I waited for a reply.

She had trouble sleeping. I started to keep my phone beside me on the pillow. It doubled as an alarm. Sometimes I would wake up, thinking I'd heard it. Sometimes I did hear it.

I'm bored.

Four more hours till the alarm goes off.

So what are you wearing?

It was childish, but it distracted me from my grief, which was not only grief about my husband but a sense of a promise I had broken, a promise made to my children by having them. Not the promise of two parents, that mirage of a steady life, unnoticed as the nail that holds up the picture. A promise that I would get it right, would surpass my own parents, who had been and were perfectly generous and capable people, within the usual limitations. They had not failed me in any spectacular way, and yet when I had children I had allowed myself to entertain the idea that I would do it better.

Do what? It.

I tried not to think that, but it was there somewhere, the furtive conviction that I would solve all the things my parents had failed to solve. Which I suppose is the same thing as saying I thought I would never experience the moment that you realize your children see through your hypocrisies and are as terrified and condemning as you were with your own parents. You shake your head at yourself, for thinking you would be spared.

I was working at the dining-room table when the phone vibrated beside me. *I found it. That's her house.* Followed by pictures, indistinct and at a distance, and an address near us. A figure on the porch, opening the door, turning to say something to the two children beside her. They were blonde, making her artificially black hair look almost purple, dulled and synthetic, a costume.

I didn't respond to the text for a few hours. I hadn't taken seriously the idea that this plan, that any of it, was real. I thought it was a conduit for friendship, like jumping from the highest point in the playground or breaking the windows in the derelict house on the neighbouring street.

Finally, I wrote back: *nice work. what next?*

At pick up, Shannon was standing among the women, the complex unspoken alliances temporarily dissolved. The man had dissolved them; perhaps we should have been grateful for feeling united, perhaps that was part of the energy on their (our: I joined them) faces, the hushed verve with which the women talked, even Shannon.

He had followed someone's babysitter home the previous night. She had only slowly become aware that he was following her. She was 16, a young 16, braces and glasses, ratty hoodie and jeans and runners, her hair artlessly slung into a ponytail. She sometimes babysat for me. I liked her but was a little bored by her: she hectored me on feminism and neo-liberalism, believing her thoughts new, that she was educating me. She had a boyfriend I suspected was gay and they played *Magic: The Gathering* together and attended Comicon. I admired her unobtrusive confidence; I admired the elaborate Comicon costumes, which seemed like evidence of someone who was sincerely pursuing a very specific, unselfconscious satisfaction. She was, at least for now, in possession of herself.

The man followed her at a distance until she started running and then he was running too, and she reached her porch and hammered on the door. Her father came out and the man kept running, his run unbroken as though he'd had no object in mind. The father made a half-hearted sprint after the man, who branched off into the park and was lost. Now no one knew what to do other than walk their daughters home. There were various opinions, offered quickly but then tailing off. There was nothing we could do because nothing definite had actually happened.

I left the schoolyard with my children and talked to them again in the offhand style I had perfected and which I imagine they saw through. I tried not to frighten them. They did their homework. I made dinner. Shannon texted: *can I come for a drink after bedtime?*

I placed two glasses on the coffee table, located cigarettes that I'd hidden in the utility drawer under folded vacuum bags and duct tape. Told my daughter not to read too long, not to have her phone in bed. Shannon was late. I thought about the man. The problem of the man, so ailing, so brutally adrift, his angry puzzled face, his mother, the brother with his motorbike, all of us in our houses, thinking of the man, our imaginations over-working, and I was so afraid. Not of the man (though that was part of it), but of all of us, of our certainty. He was frightening; I knew that. He could not be explained away. He was real. But I was nearly as frightened of our surge of fellow-feeling, talking about him in the yard. How richly alive I'd felt, in a way that had, if I was honest, very little to do with the girl, with her body hurtling down the sidewalk, and everything to do with the feeling of crisis and the cohesion it gave us. I was sick of myself, and I wasn't ready for Shannon, who let herself in. I'd made myself leave the door unlocked in some kind of futile private pact about trust.

Shannon threw herself down on the couch, tossed her coat on the chair opposite her, and poured the wine clumsily, licking at the rivulet going down her wrist. She wore a long yellow dress and brown high-heeled boots with laces up to the top and looked like a cartoon of herself. She flexed one leg, pointing her toe at me.

"I got dressed up. We were supposed to go out, but then he had too much work to do. And Chloe was supposed to babysit, but her mother thinks she's not ready yet, so he said we should just cancel. It's not like he knows how to find another babysitter anyway. So I sent the kids to bed and left."

She pouted, drawing in her foot.

"I know I'm supposed to be supportive but I wish he would just get an assistant or something for the paperwork. It's insane that he still does it himself. It's like the way he is about money, worrying about everything and going over everything five times."

"How's Chloe?"

She sipped her wine, mulish, very different from her expression in the yard.

"Oh, she'll be fine. She's just had a scare. It's not a big deal."

Her mouth turned down in what I thought was a reassertion of cynicism and then suspected was hurt that I had not taken the opening, asking her, jokingly enough that she could ignore me if she wanted, about her husband. She never talked about him. We'd spent too much time together for me to admit I didn't remember his name. I saw something else, too, in the flick of her tongue along her wrist, in the way she sat down and tossed away her coat, that reminded me of myself buying the green boots and talking too loudly. It made me want to be her friend, her real friend, not in this whispering way as though we hoped someone would overhear, someone we wished to shock or ostracize. I wanted to know about her life. I wanted to remember her husband's name and her birthday and I wanted her to be someone with whom I didn't have to be funny and cutting and coy, someone I relied on to talk me down from my own ledges. But I couldn't figure out how to begin.

Marvin. That was his name. She said it. She'd said it before, but I confused it with her son, Matthew. Of course they wouldn't name a child Marvin, it was not one of those 19th century names that had come back, like Thomas, Charlotte, Hazel, James, Olive, and Violet, hinting at a life of curling photographs and dead flowers. Shannon puffed noisily, looked up at me.

"What?" she asked.

"Nothing. Just a weird day."

"Yeah."

"I'm tired. Sorry."

"Come help me get drunk."

I sat down on the far side of the couch. She tipped her head back into the light that hung above her, shut her eyes. In the glare from the halogen bulb her face was drawn tight, slack under her chin. Her eyelids gashed with dark shadow, applied a little too thickly, moving up to her brows. I waited for her to open her eyes. She angled her chin back even farther, straining to keep her mouth closed, drew slow circles in the air with her nose.

"I'm tired, too," she said.

She wanted me to ask why. I didn't know how to ask her anything, and the inept smudges on her eyelids unsettled me, as though she were deranged and I'd never noticed, because I was too, and the women, the other women, had a certain scepticism about us both because they sensed what I couldn't. I had no sense. We'd recognized each other as mutually close to shipwreck, but I was always late to realize why I'd done a thing, wanted something or someone, pushed someone away. I hadn't known my husband would leave until he left, and then when he left I thought he would come back. But if Shannon was a wreck, I would be too. I didn't want to be left.

"Let's go look at the house."

She opened her eyes.

"What?"

"If you found the address. We'll just look."

"Why?"

"Don't you want to see it?"

"I don't know. Do I?"

"Sure you do," I said, "of course you do."

Once, when my children were small, I was watching TV with my husband, some show about the *Titanic* that neither of us cared about very much. We made fun of it together, pointing out anachronisms, superfluous subplots. It was close to the end: icy water, final goodbyes, screams, tears. Underneath it

I heard a faint wailing but thought it was from the screen, some background added for effect, an unseen agony at the fact of dying coming from one of the portals, and I was discomfited and even moved, without saying so, by the high thin sound, the genuine despair. It was my husband who realized that it was our children, two and nearly four. We ran upstairs. The door to their room didn't hang true and sometimes jammed. One had woken, woken the other, they'd screamed for us and no one came. They'd climbed out of bed and tried to get the door open. We didn't come. They were locked in the room, left alone. We'd gone away and deserted them and there was no escape.

I wrenched the door open and they ran out, tumbling over each other. We picked them up and told them how sorry we were, how sorry, and they screamed and screamed until they were quiet, shuddering, as we tried to convince them that we were good and that they were safe. And they were convinced. They were young enough to be convinced.

We each held a child. I was more shaken than the event deserved. As if that was the first moment of faltering, that I had heard them and not heard them. As though they were not mine and I could not help them. I could not help anything.

The next morning Shannon followed me to the address she'd found. She walked a little behind me. All attempts at talking faltered. I felt as if I'd hurt her, unless I was seeing another hurt, one I knew nothing about, which would not prevent me guessing what it was. She would require some kind of grandiose folly, some abasement, as proof of loyalty. She trailed behind me and I thought about love, and spacious foolhardy gestures, and that I couldn't make anyone come back.

We stood across the street.

Shannon said nothing.

I stepped into the street.

"Where are you going? What are you doing?"

"I'm going to knock on the door."

"What? Are you crazy?"

I crossed the street.

"This is crazy!" Shannon called, looking around to see if anyone was watching us.

"Come on!"

"This is crazy. You're crazy."

I went up the steps.

At the door, I looked back. Shannon had gone. I could just see her, walking, then running down the street toward her own house, and then I saw the man, passing her on one of his walks, as if nothing had happened, as if no one was afraid of him or had any reason to be. He came toward me as Shannon ran away from me and I didn't blame her, I'd run away from me too. But I'd go this far, so I waited till the man was across the street where he could see me and I made a fist and lifted my hand.

Joe Bongiorno

SUGARLAND

Yves Dubois counts the rusty barrels in the back of the truck's cargo trailer. "Twenty-two, just like Laurent said," he mutters under his breath. He glances at the time on his phone. It's already past midnight; the job is taking longer than expected. He wants to get the delivery over with. Sweat trickles down his forehead as he locks the cargo trailer doors and hobbles toward the tractor unit, nearly slipping on the ice.

The windshield sparkles. Ice crystals cover the glass, spread out like frozen spruce needles. He scrapes off the frost with the chisel end of the snowbrush, careful not to put pressure on the gnarled itchy growths on his limbs. He feels like ripping off his toque and the garbage bags wrapped around his arms, but he cannot afford to attract any attention. With his condition, he would be the most identifiable man in the country, a sketch artist's fantasy.

Yves gets into the driver's seat, turns the key in the ignition, and hits the gas. Seven hundred kilometres to go. Until he reaches Grand Falls, the future of the family business – what remains of it – lies in the back of his truck. He shifts the vehicle into gear and merges onto the main road, watching in the side mirror as the shrivelling maples of the Dubois sugar bush dissolve into black and white.

How long will it take the federation – or, as the Dubois sons call them, *le cartel* – to figure out that 22 barrels worth over sixty-seven thousand dollars have gone missing from their Reineville warehouse?

—⁊⋏⋍—

"*Réveille-toi,*" Yves commands himself, forcing his eyes wide open with a yawn. "Wake up! Only a hundred kilometres on the road and you're already nodding off." He turns a corner on the winding highway, both hands gripping the wheel. In his daydream, the truck swerves into the median and flips onto its side, barrels bursting open, slathering the road with a sweet, sticky substance and ensnaring curious deer by their hooves.

The phone rings. Yves rubs his eyes and looks down at the number. It's Fleurant, his eldest brother, the one waiting for the drop-off at a Grand Falls motel. Between Fleurant's nerves and Laurent's hot head, Yves considers letting the call go to voice-mail, but then decides against it, knowing Fleurant will keep calling until he picks up.

Yves clears his throat and sticks out his chest, preparing to answer with the feigned confidence of a man in control. "Hello?"

"Where are you?" Fleurant blurts.

"Just passed Saint-Romuald. Crossing the river."

"The buyer should be here within the next hour. Any word?"

"Not yet," Yves answers. He thinks of Laurent, the middle brother, who's back in Sugarland on the lookout for signs of heat. It was he who, over the course of three weeks, had loaded the truck with *le cartel*'s warehouse reserve barrels during the night.

"Okay," Fleurant sighs, telegraphing his unease. "Pick up the pace."

Yves hangs up, replaying the events that have led up to the heist.

As one-third of the operation, he's the youngest of three sons to inherit the centuries-old sugar bush. "See, you're a natural," Yves remembers his father saying the first time he had taken him into the woods to learn the trade. "You chose a good tree. Now, stick the drill in and make a hole." Yves had watched in excitement as the sap had trickled from the spile into the pail and had stuck out his tongue for a taste. "Not done just yet," his father had laughed, puffing on a cigarette. "Now we gotta cook it down and filter out the sugar sand."

Production began plummeting after peaking in the previous decade. For the fifth consecutive year, their maples had been devastated by gusts, ice, bark beetles, and heavy metals. One bad harvest after another, strangling the business, the losses wiping away the savings of the three brothers. The trees, and the men, tapped dry.

Fleurant had resisted filing for bankruptcy. "Dead-end," he had called it one January afternoon. He had then declared that burning their facility down for the insurance money amounted to "destroying our legacy."

Laurent had interrupted, hunching forward on the kitchen table, his gut slumping onto the oak. "I say we hit *le cartel*. Remember all the barrels they stole from us? Those were our best years! What have they done to help us out of the red? Nothing, that's what. I say those pricks have it coming."

"What are you proposing?" Fleurant had asked, cleaning his ear with a Q-tip. He crossed his long, lean legs and flicked the cotton swab into the trash can.

"I know someone on the inside," Laurent had explained. "There are still producers out there on the other side of the

Saint Lawrence making money. Their maples weren't turned to shit like ours. My contact says there are tons of barrels at the warehouse."

Fleurant's blue eyes had lit up. "I know someone out east who might be interested. If you can get your hands on some sugar."

Yves had agreed. Though the last thing he wanted to do was add legal trouble to their plight, there was no way of backing out with his elder brothers on board. Was he supposed to sit back and watch their sugar bush rot? The decades-old memory of *le cartel* forcing them to give up their surplus syrup still felt fresh. The Dubois regularly defied the federation's quota limits. Their father, now dead from diabetes after years of slathering syrup on everything, had insisted their syrup was never *le cartel*'s to control.

⁓ノ↖⁓

Yves stares into the snowy darkness of the road ahead. *Drip. Drip.* His nose begins to leak. The run-off pools onto his upper lip; it tastes sugary and sappy – the "sweet bleeds." He wipes it off with his plastic-wrapped arm while steering with his free hand. Since hitting puberty two decades ago, his nose has been dripping every year between late winter and early spring, coinciding with harvest season. Strapped for cash, he started boiling, bottling and selling his generous flowing sap at an artisanal farmers' market. The side hustle was none of his brothers' business, he'd decided. The sweet bleeds weren't their problem, and certainly not their profit.

For a decade, he had held on to the hope that his leaky nose was the result of seasonal allergies, but his *grand-maman* Yvonne had crossed her twiggy arms and shaken her head.

"Our heritage isn't an allergy. Mine was just like yours not so long ago," she said, pointing to her long, craggy nose. When she exhaled, black nose hairs spun in the air like double-winged samaras in autumn.

More sap trickles down. He wipes some off, but it pours down his chin, then onto his jacket and jeans. Securing the steering the wheel with his knees, Yves searches the glove compartment for something to stem the flow, but the only thing he can find is a wad of Canadian Tire money. He crumples a 50-cent bill and stuffs it up his snub nose only to sneeze out the paper in a new wave of sap.

From the corner of his eye, Yves spots a Tim Hortons on the side of the highway, its *Ouvert 24 hrs* sign glowing in red neon. *Toujours frais.* Though he knows he can't afford to make any stops, he refuses to let his nose leak all the way to New Brunswick. Besides, he needs some caffeine to get through the snowy, moonlit winter morning. "If Fleurant doesn't like it, he can do the driving himself next time," Yves says. "He can fall asleep behind the wheel, for all I care."

Yves gets off at the exit, goes around the overpass, and turns into the restaurant parking lot. He gets down from the driver's seat and rushes inside, slowing down near the entrance to avoid arousing suspicion. He wheezes, his breathing becoming more laboured in recent months as his left leg has stiffened and his flesh has hardened. Covering his nose with his plastic-wrapped hand, he hobbles past the beaming clerk, who looks up at him from a fresh batch of maple-glaze donuts. Her smile twists into a grimace, and she reaches up to touch the bun of her hair, done up neatly in a hairnet. A truck driver seated alone at a booth eyes him as he heads straight for the bathroom. Old news, Yves thinks, long the recipient of every variety of dirty look and prying stare.

Yves locks the bathroom door and blows his nose, filling one paper towel after the next with sap until the sweet bleeds stop flowing. He removes his toque and scratches the rough, bark-like surface of his scalp, nearly tearing out the forever-itching saplings sprouting amid his curls. He then removes the garbage bags wrapped around his arms. The deeply rooted warts on his forearms ache. If not for the heist he would not have bothered covering them up. Even when he gets the warts surgically removed, they grow right back. The knobby growths on his fingers have sprouted a good inch in the past few months. When he was young, doctors had diagnosed him with *epidermodysplasia verruciformis*, the rare "treeman syndrome," but *grand-maman* Yvonne had shaken her head once more.

"*Mon ti-fils*, it's just a part of your inheritance," she had explained. "It skips a generation. Don't envy your moron brothers." Before she had laid down her roots for good, she'd warned him not to forget his own. "In ancient Greece, people were always turning into elms and poplars. What's the big deal?"

—)|(—

The sun teases from the maritime horizon, tucked beneath the not-so-distant New Brunswick border. Yves knocks back the last of his coffee and crushes the plastic-coated cup. Making good time, he thinks, steadily increasing his speed. Two hours to go.

Yves daydreams about getting rid of the cargo and cracks a smile of relief. He fantasizes about going his own way, selling his sweet bleed syrup and maple-glazed Danishes in the city. And if the syrup business is dying, why not chop down their sugar bush and sell the lumber? He pictures fine dining tables and chairs being carved from the wood. Furniture replete with flourishes, regal fleurs-de-lys fit for the governor of New France.

Then, without warning, the flow of traffic slows to a crawl. The brake lights of the fruit truck ahead of him glow red. The van behind him honks. Bumper to bumper. Yves and his cargo are brought to a near-standstill. Three lanes restricted to one. What's the next exit? Rivière-du-Loup?

Yves sticks his head out the window, but he can't see anything past the vehicles ahead of him. Construction, he figures, though strangely enough for Quebec, he hasn't seen any pylons for kilometres. "I don't have time for this," he mumbles, eying the dashboard clock just as the sweet bleeds resume their flow.

The fruit truck ahead of him creeps forward. Yves peeks out of the window again and sees a roadblock ahead. "*Merde*," he curses, heart pounding at the sight of police officers. A short female cop with a ponytail is speaking to the driver of a hatchback. Too early for a sobriety check, he thinks, probably just a car wreck, but his chest tightens when he sees her inspect the trunk. All clear. She waves the car on.

Yves wipes his nose, considering what to do next. He checks his phone. No missed calls. He pretends not to notice the officer in the fur earflap cap, standing by a police cruiser, staring at him. The police have always given him a hard time on account of his condition. In fact, he has gotten used to being pulled over for no apparent reason, but that was without sixty-seven thousand dollars in stolen syrup in the trunk. He thinks of calling Laurent. No time for that, he decides. As the female cop moves on to the driver hauling fruit ahead of him, he realizes that he has to make a decision: stay put or abandon the truck. He glances at the snow-blanketed firs and pines on the side of the highway.

The ponytailed cop points to the driver's trailer and makes her way to check the cargo. The fruit truck driver unlocks his trailer doors, and she scans its contents. Too many vehicles to plough through the roadblock, Yves decides, not that he can get far with his truck. He imagines himself being questioned, stammering, unable to answer for the cargo as they drag him to the station. He makes his choice; it's too late to save the wilting maples of their sugar bush.

While the officer in the fur cap looks at the fruit truck and speaks into the walkie talkie, Yves slips on his gloves and toque, nudges opens the door, and sneaks out of the cabin. Forcing the dead weight of his left leg to move, he turns behind the cover of his vehicle and jumps, falls over the safety barrier into the roadside woods. With a good head start, he can lose his tail before they figure out which way he has gone.

A ray of sunlight slices through the purple-orange sky, illuminating the snow between the red and silver maples. He struggles through the deep snow. Despite his inexplicable resistance to cold – the only perk of his condition – the shrieking wind stings the parts of his skin not covered in warts and growths. For a quarter of an hour, he pushes through the falling snow, slowed down by its depth. Yves hunches over a rock to catch his breath, panting. His twisted legs can only take him so far. With sap streaming from his nose onto his boots, he breathes through his mouth.

Any minute now, Fleurant will call, inquiring about his whereabouts, checking up on him. Can his calls be traced, used as evidence against them in court? He considers smashing his phone against a rock and burying it under the snow. If he can make it to the other side of the woods to a gas station, he can call his brothers from a payphone. Wouldn't they do the same for him? He imagines Fleurant breathing hard and Laurent losing his temper, planting his boot into a wall.

Yves turns his head and sees the amber trail of sap that leads straight to where he stands. His fingerprints are on the wheel. "*Tabarnac*," he mutters. When he tries to move, he discovers that he is stuck. The sap has frozen him into place. He is too tired to struggle. The sweet bleeds have congealed into tusk-sized icicles, and more is rushing through his nasal cavity, backed up like pipes soon to burst. He tries to devise a new plan, a way to break the news to his brothers, but pressure is steadily building in his forehead.

The sun rises above the treetops. Yves squints in the glaring light. A chirping chickadee lands on his shoulder and pecks at the frozen sap hanging from his chin. He shrugs, but the bird patters across his back to the other shoulder and pecks away. Another bird lands on his ear, a third at his feet. He wants to yell, to curse his inheritance, but he can only muster a moan like branches swaying in the wind.

Beth Goobie

ONE YEAR

Cassie ducked her head and put more burn into her pedalling. The main challenge that came with biking in Holland, she was quickly learning, was the endless wind – without hills, there was nothing to slow it down. And all those picturesque canals meant the wind was jam-packed with bugs, an insect's version of the ride of the Valkyries. A cyclist had to keep her mouth shut and avoid breathing through her nose – an impossible task. Tears stung Cassie's eyes and she blinked fiercely. *Yes, an impossible task.*

At least it wasn't raining. And today she had encountered little traffic on this rural road. Saturday afternoon must have everyone migrating to Rotterdam, 20 kilometres west. A few cows raised their heads and blessed her with their mild gaze as she cycled by. She had seen a heifer once, stuck in a canal and bawling its head off as, 10 feet to its right, vehicles sped past. The Dutch were an efficient people; they got to where they needed to go. To them, she was the "*meisje vanuit Canada,*" learning the ropes.

Up ahead a church came into view, along with a pebble-stoned driveway and a small surrounding cemetery. Cassie turned off the road, slowing to manage the slip-slide gravel, and dismounted from the heavy black bike her employers had loaned her. The bike was so solid, it felt as if it belonged to the World War II era, which would make it 30-plus years old. Back in Canada, kids were cruising around on banana seats and watching *Happy Days*. Ditching the bike against the waist-high stone wall that enclosed the place, Cassie wandered through the open cemetery gate. As on her earlier visits, the century-old church appeared deserted. She had yet to see anyone coming or going from it.

Cassie crossed to the cemetery's far side, away from the church entrance, where she sat down under a poplar to eat her lunch – a Gouda cheese sandwich and a *stroopwafel*. She had her weekends off and her employers made no claim on her then, at least not in her role as au pair. Eyes closed, she savoured the rich mild texture of the Gouda. Her head ached; she hadn't been sleeping well. Since her arrival a month ago, an invisible heaviness had settled onto her. Her bones felt as if they were made of stone; sometimes it was such an effort to breathe. Three months earlier, she had graduated from an Ontario high school with both academic and citizenship awards – transatlantic significance that hadn't followed her here.

She took a slow swallow of the orange juice she had purchased at a store on the edge of town. As she was leaving the house, Jap had offered her a bottle of mineral water, with a wink and that smug smile that felt as if it had hands; Cassie had dumped it down the sink as soon as he had left the kitchen. There was something about the drinks he had been giving her of late – nothing she could pinpoint, things just seemed to get blurry after the first few sips. But then everything felt blurred these days, inside her head and out. Maybe it was just Jap's smile she didn't trust. And the way Tena's pale blue eyes never quite met hers.

Cassie had taken this job, travelled to another continent to work as a nanny for people she had never met, based on the recommendation of their relatives – a family she knew from her church at home. Both of her new employers worked – Tena as a social worker and Jap as the personal assistant to the mayor of a nearby city. Back in Canada, the job offer had seemed a dream come true – one year in Europe with an income, before she returned to Ontario to start university. Back in Canada, it hadn't occurred to her to question why Dutch parents would prefer to hire an English-speaking nanny sight unseen for their Dutch-speaking children, rather than someone local, who would be familiar with the language and customs.

Thoughts shifted in her head like bodies in a dark room. Cassie went over her options again. She could call home, tell her parents it wasn't working out and ask them to send her a ticket home. She wouldn't have to tell the truth, just say she couldn't handle it. But even without picking up the phone, Cassie could hear her mother's voice, bewildered, disappointed. Her mother had Tena's gaze, sidestepping, sliding away from contact. What she didn't want to see, she didn't see; Cassie had grown up learning what made her visible and what cast her out into the void. A panicky phone call requesting money would be void material – as the oldest of four children, her departure from the family budget had been a welcome relief. But more importantly, if she came back prematurely there would be the question of why, and in her home no one asked why, especially her mother.

"Oh, you're just a little down, Cass," she would say, her voice rising into its high-anxiety pitch. "Have you prayed about this?"

The kids were cute – just two of them, like most of the other families on the street. Unlike most of the other wives, however, Tena commuted from their village row house to Rotterdam for work. From what Cassie had observed, feminists were in short supply in Dutch village life. Not that she was a bra-burner, herself, but still… Again, tears burned acid into Cassie's eyes. If it weren't for the kids, she couldn't bear it.

It had been a week since the conversation. The kids had been put to bed and she, Jap, and Tena had sat down to the customary late dinner in front of the TV. But this time the TV wasn't switched on. Jap and Tena engaged in their usual stilted conversation in English to ensure Cassie felt included, Jap holding centre stage, Tena playing up to him with her admiring laugh and downcast eyes. Then came the pause in conversation, some new intention shouldering into the silence. Hairs lifted on the back of Cassie's neck.

Tena's voice was casually lightweight. "Something has gone missing," she said, not looking up.

Jap glanced at her, his expression neutral. "What's that?" he asked.

"My grandmother's gold watch that she left to me," said Tena. "Or, let me think – is it money? Five hundred guilders that I left in my dresser? No, no – that sapphire necklace you gave me for our anniversary, Jap."

Jap's eyebrows ascended. "Anything else you can think of?" he asked.

"The silver plate," replied Tena. "I think – the sugar and cream set."

Cassie's heart thundered, her gaze flitting between her employers like a trapped bird. She had spent hours the previous day polishing the silverware, and of course she had put everything back. It hadn't occurred to her to take anything. She *wouldn't*.

"A sugar and cream set that *could* go missing, I think you mean," said Jap. "It hasn't yet."

"You are right," Tena conceded. "Not yet."

Cassie's innards had dissolved into cold sludge. She wanted to speak but her throat had gone solid with panic, her tongue a dead thing in her mouth. A knock sounded at the front door. Without glancing at Cassie, Jap got up to answer it. While he was gone, Tena sat gazing at the floor while Cassie stared mutely at her employer's lowered head. Jovial male voices sounded in the kitchen, then entered the living room. As Jap returned to his seat on the couch beside Tena, an older man sat down in an armchair facing Cassie. He was wearing a police officer's uniform.

Shock crashed soundless cymbals in Cassie's brain. Had they reported her already? But they had just said the cream and sugar set hadn't gone missing. So was this about the gold watch or the sapphire necklace? She hadn't taken them either, she hadn't stolen anything! Theft was stupid; it was boring. Who wanted to go through life snatching stuff? Who cared about *stuff?*

"Officer Oesterveldt, thank you for dropping by," Jap said to the police officer in a light, even tone. "We have a problem, you see. Well, we *might* have a problem, we'll have to see. It's all in how you look at things, *jahoor*, Tena?"

"Oh *ja*," she agreed.

The three Dutch adults nodded and spoke benignly to each other in English. No one glanced at Cassie. Rigid, body-slammed by heartbeat, Cassie sat staring into her own vanishing point.

"What is the penalty for stealing a valuable sapphire necklace?" asked Jap. "In the law, here in Holland?"

Officer Oesterveldt leaned back in the armchair and pursed his lips. "Oh, a year, maybe two years," he said. "Theft is no joking matter in this country. The problem, really, is the backlog. The jails are crowded. You can sit in there six months just to get a trial date set. Then you have to wait for the trial. And then, after all that, you serve the sentence."

"And if it's someone foreign," asked Jap. "The accused?"

"Oh, then there is no bail," Officer Oesterveldt said firmly. "They might try to run, you see."

"And if the accused did try to run – say, buy a plane ticket out of Holland?" Jap mused.

For the first time, Officer Oesterveldt looked directly at Cassie. A slight smile played his mouth, smug, knowing. "We have records of passports," he said, savouring each word. "The airports are covered. All you have to do is show it and—" He snapped his fingers. "We've got you."

The finger-snap ran through Cassie like electric shock. She stared into the officer's gun-barrel gaze, trying to find her voice in the lostness of her throat.

"To run like that, and buy a ticket," said Tena, studying the carpet. "It would look guilty, no?"

Officer Oesterveldt chuckled. "*Very* guilty," he assured her.

Apparently finished with the topic, the three started once again conversing as if Cassie were incidental to the scene – a table lamp, a bag of *zoutjes*. They exchanged comments about family and the weather, and then the two men stood and Jap escorted the officer out. Tena and Cassie sat motionless, without speaking, until Jap returned. As before, he sat beside his wife, his face in its usual congenial lines as he turned to Cassie.

"So you understand the situation," he said calmly. "Things could go missing at any time. If they do, certain events will follow. We are just letting you know, to save you the trouble." He paused a moment, gazing into a future only he could see, then returned his untroubled eyes to her. "We have an organization," he continued. "We do not speak of it beyond ourselves. We will begin training you for service in the next few days. If you let yourself enjoy it, you will have a good time. It's all about having a good time – there is nothing to be afraid of. But you must understand, you will never speak of it. Not while you are here, or after – when you leave." Without the slightest change in expression, Jap raised his right hand and drew it across his throat.

"Never," he had added, his gaze bland and empty, his slight smile fixed.

Sitting with her back to the cemetery wall, Cassie felt the slight pressure of a finger cross her own throat. She swallowed convulsively, and a shudder ran through her. Since the conversation a week ago, she had been running through different possibilities like a rat in a maze; they had all resulted in the same dead end. She was so tired, even her lungs felt weary. She rubbed her wrists, which were beginning to chafe from the tie ropes. *Training:* her cheeks burned, molten at the memories.

A single white swan flew overhead; Cassie followed it with her eyes. She had seen one, dead in a canal, on a recent bike ride… or perhaps it had recovered and there it was now, athrill with the possibilities of sky. *Not likely.* With a moan, she slid her stiff legs under her butt and rolled onto her knees, then rose to her feet. Slowly, she walked across the pebbly yard to a grave near the church's front door – a stone cross with the photo of a woman at its centre. Decades of sunlight had faded the photo to contrasts of grey; the woman wore a floor-length dress and her hair was pulled back into a chignon. She appeared to be in her late 20s, an ordinary-looking woman except for her protuberant eyes, which stared directly at the camera.

"Fish eyes" was what kids called them back in Ontario. Cassie guessed this woman had carried a similar burden of taunts, contemporary to her own time period. It was difficult to determine from the ageing photo if her expression was defiant or defeated, but although the picture had been taken while she was alive, and from the looks of it healthy, something about the eyes gave them the appearance of gazing back from beyond the grave.

Cassie had first spotted this photo four days ago on an earlier bike ride; the gaze of those eyes was what had drawn her back here today. She stood a long time in the ache of her body, observing it. Men's voices faded in and out of her thoughts, telling her she liked it, asking her to smile, she had a pretty face, a lovely body. But her body felt bloated, ugly with experiences she could not name. She had left home to escape nights with a father that no one would talk about; when she returned, one year from now, it would not be to Ontario. She would go to a place where she knew no one, where she would trust no one. There, she would make her way, watching the world through a dead woman's eyes.

Jennifer DeLeskie

OCOSINGO

On Lee's fifth night in Comalapa, shortly after dinner, Padre
Diego burst through Cristina and Paolo's door with a bottle of
mezcal, poured shots for everyone, and proceeded to teach her
how to conjugate the verb *chingar. Yo chingo, tu chingas, nosotros
chingamos.* I fuck, you fuck, we all fuck. They spent the evening
sitting around Cristina and Paolo's small Formica table, listening to Cuban folk music on an ancient CD player and passing
around a joint. Nobody made any special effort to speak
English, so Lee had mainly listened, picking up what she could.
A mudslide up in the mountains had buried a family of seven.
A nine-year-old in Comitán had gone blind after playing with
a canister of pesticide. Doña Arceli's 15-year-old daughter had
given birth to a baby with a partially closed esophagus and the
family wanted the parish to pay for an operation. But there
were other things wrong with the baby, too. When the first
joint was done, Padre Diego passed his baggie of weed to Paolo,
who rolled a second. Padre Diego said he was going to
Ocosingo the next day for meetings – a five- or six-hour drive
– and invited Lee to join him. Lee looked at Cristina, who
smiled and shrugged. She trusted Cristina, even though they
had only met a few days earlier and communicated mainly
through gestures, so she accepted the invitation. Besides,
Ocosingo sounded promising. The name evoked whitewashed

homes with terracotta roofs, walls draped with bougainvillea, and women in bright *huipils* carrying baskets of calla lilies.

But later, as she lay in her cot in Cristina and Paolo's chicken shed, Lee began to have second thoughts. She tried to imagine Father Pat, her high-school chaplain, smoking a joint and making jokes about fucking, and found that she could not. Then again, Father Pat had probably never picked bodies out of a mudslide or comforted a nine-year-old who'd gone blind. Maybe proximity to tragedy allowed one to bend the rules a little. Maybe Padre Diego got to smoke weed and teach a young *gringa* volunteer how to conjugate *chingar* because Doña Arceli's granddaughter was going to die.

Lee woke early the next morning and slipped out of Cristina and Paolo's house before sunrise, giving herself extra time to walk to the rectory in case she got lost along the way. She was surprised to find the bodega next door open and Doña Lety at her station, seated in front of a small TV that spilled colour and noise onto the dark and otherwise quiet street. Cristina had taken Lee to meet Doña Lety on her first night, and Lee guessed that the matronly woman and her bodega were the beating heart of the neighbourhood. They'd sat in the courtyard sipping Fantas while Doña Lety's two young grand-daughters hung off Lee, alternating between shy and boister-ous. Lee French-braided their hair and taught them English words for things around them: cat, television, oven, plastic pail, barrette, pink, nose, eyelashes, princess. That night Lee had fallen asleep suffused with the sense that the encounter had been a meaningful one.

Now she considered the packaged junk displayed on Doña Lety's counter and selected a cellophane-wrapped *big-ote de cajeta*, a sort of Mexican Twinkie. *Esperate*, Doña Lety said as Lee finished paying. Wait. The woman hissed and her lean yellow dog, Rabo, roused himself from the dirt floor and trotted out the door, tail wagging like a metronome. *Para caminar contigo,* Dona Lety said. To walk with you. The unexpected kindness made heat prickle behind Lee's eyes. Rabo would know his way along the unmarked streets of low cinder block and stucco buildings, indistinguishable from each other save for the ubiquitous political slogans and inexpert murals of pigs, chickens, and children that adorned their surfaces. Rabo would protect her from the packs of feral dogs that roamed the town and the drunks who gathered outside the cantina at all hours, hissing *güera, güera* – white girl – as she passed.

Lee and Padre Diego arrived in Ocosingo before noon. It turned out to be a dirty sprawl of a city, clogged with tuk-tuks and street vendors selling plastic crap. Lee abandoned her plan of exploring the town on her own and tagged along with Padre Diego, feeling as useless and conspicuous as a hood ornament. As the day wore on, she grew exhausted from her efforts at understanding the conversation around her, at smiling and being an object of curiosity and, she thought, mild disapproval because, in her cut-off jeans and crop top, she wasn't remotely appropriately dressed. Padre Diego seemed to have business with everyone in town: at the city hall, the local office of the coffee cooperative, and the *comida* corridor where they ate lunch. Yet, despite his pressing engagements, he moved leisurely, like a planet, dabbing sweat from his face with a bandana and steering Lee through the crowded streets with a light touch on her elbow. He towered over everyone, even Lee, who was herself tall and had to duck under awnings at the market, which sold pigs' heads and live chickens instead of the flowers and crafts she had imagined. Aside from the cross he wore on a leather cord around his neck, Padre Diego bore no signs of his office, but the locals, small, wiry men in rubber sandals and women with round, pleasant faces, treated him solicitously. *A sus órdenes, a sus órdenes*, they said, stepping aside to make room for him on the sidewalk, or offering to shine his cowboy boots. The evening before, he'd pointed to those boots and told Lee he was from Sonora. Now Lee thought she understood what he had meant; he was practically an American, almost the same as her.

The sun was sinking behind the mountains when they finally started back. Lee rode shotgun, clutching a can of Tecate from the six-pack Padre Diego bought at the service station when he filled up the truck. The road was bad, pocked with holes and speedbumps, and several times an animal – a dog or a goat – appeared in the headlights like a phantom. Each time Lee sucked air through her teeth, and each time Padre Diego laughed and said, *No te preocupes*. Don't worry. He drove too fast, taking swigs from his beer – his second or maybe his third – and it occurred to Lee that he was showing off for her, trying to impress the *gringa* who'd attended meetings on combatting erosion in the *cafetales* dressed for a day at the beach.

This is an adventure, Lee reminded herself, trying to stop the worried running of her mind. She imagined bragging to friends back home – friends she did not, in truth, have at that moment – *Did I ever tell you about the time I worked in Chiapas with a Marxist priest who drank beer and smoked weed?* Her stories would be saturated with wild and irreverent anecdotes, and her friends, those nameless and faceless admirers, would marvel at her doings. As she was luxuriating in this idea of herself, they passed a whitewashed cross, the 20th or maybe the 30th of the day. They were becoming part of the landscape, these crosses, commemorating other people's tragedies, but not hers.

The mountains they drove toward were negative spaces, outlined in thinning bands of light. Paolo, an agronomist, told

Lee on her first day that their terraced slopes were an ecological and human disaster, deforested and eroded, dotted with villages that lacked everything. But from a distance the mountains looked magical; round and symmetrical, like mountains in a children's book. Lee accepted a second beer. By the time she was three-quarters finished, they'd begun climbing up into the range, and the beer had started spreading warmth along her limbs. The stars blinked on one by one until the night squirmed with dancing pinpricks of light. Lee opened the window and leaned a little way out, breathing in air that held within it a trace of burning. The radio station finally stabilized, and a wistful voice accompanied by guitar sang *Rayando el sol, rayando por ti*. It was an earnest song, one Lee would have been embarrassed to listen to back home, but at that moment it was beautiful. Perfect, even. Lee finished the beer, kicked off her shoes, and propped her feet up on the dashboard, unfurling a long and pale expanse of leg. She caught Padre Diego glancing at them, and immediately wished she could draw them back into her body.

A quick, low shape materialized in the headlights. Padre Diego yanked the wheel and Lee was thrown against the side of the truck. There was a thump, small and solid. Then they smacked into something harder, and the truck spun out into the centre of the road, juddering to a stop mere inches from the guardrail.

Pinche perro, Padre Diego said. Fucking dog. He flipped on the hazards and coaxed the truck to other side of the road, away from the drop off, each rotation of the tires accompanied by a nauseating lurch. When the truck was nestled against the rock face, he turned off the engine, reached across Lee, and pulled a flashlight from the glove compartment. Then he heaved himself out of the truck.

Lee sat for a moment longer, taking rapid, fractured breaths, unsure if she had escaped calamity. Then she opened Padre Diego's door – there wasn't enough clearance to open the door on her side – and exited the truck. A small, light-coloured heap lay in the middle of the road. Lee went over to it, squatting and stretching out her hand. A dog lay in the centre of a spreading patch of darkness. It raised its head a few inches off the ground, as if trying to connect with her palm, then let it drop with a whimper.

It's still alive, Lee said in English. The dog. It's alive.

Padre Diego came and stood over her, large and solid as the mountain. *Nada para hacer*, he said. There is nothing to do. He took her by the arm, pulled her up, and began leading her back toward the truck.

Lee resisted, pulling against him. Where she was from, dogs weren't left to die by the side of the road. *Tenemos que hacer algo*, she said, hoping she had strung the words together correctly. We have to do something. Padre Diego sighed. At first Lee thought he was going to refuse to help the dog, but then he said, *Quédate aquí* – stay here – and walked back over to it.

Lee closed her eyes and listened to the sound of Padre Diego's feet crunching over the gravel. A moment later there was a dull thud that set off sparks behind her eyelids. Then she heard something crash into the scrub on the other side of the guardrail. Lee's throat constricted, and her heart began to drum arrhythmically in her chest. Of course he'd killed it. What had she expected? *Nada para hacer*.

Padre Diego returned and embraced her, clucking his tongue the way one might to soothe a baby, ignoring her rigid posture. She longed to be elsewhere. Back at Cristina and Paolo's, or sitting in Doña Lety's courtyard with her two little granddaughters on her lap. Mostly, though, she longed to be home, even though, at 22, she didn't exactly have one. No home, and no plans to do anything other than what she was doing, which wasn't exactly running away, but was close. She began to weep, and this caused Padre Diego to hug her even tighter. How had she arrived here, she wondered, stranded on a dark and dangerous road with a stranger, having just helped to cause the death of an innocent dog?

Padre Diego called a repair service, but they wouldn't come until the morning, so they had to spend the night on the mountain. It was cold, and Lee was badly underdressed. Padre Diego invited her to warm herself against him – at least, she thought this was what he was suggesting by spreading his arm and patting his chest – but the idea of pressing herself against him repelled her. She shrank against the passenger side of the truck's cab, hugged her knees to her chest, and fell into a shallow and unpleasant sleep.

At first, Lee didn't notice the hand on her thigh. She was having a night terror. The devil was grasping her, squid-like, from below, and the hand on her thigh felt like just another one of its appendages. But then it started kneading her flesh in a jarringly solid way, inching upwards after every four or five squeezes. Gradually, Lee also became aware of warm breathing on her neck. She emerged into a state of confusion, shreds of the night terror floating around inside her head like fluff.

She remembered the dog first and a strangled moan rose in her chest. Then she remembered everything else. All the while, Padre Diego's hand continued its slow creep up her thigh. Lee glanced down at it, careful not to betray her wakeful state lest she consign herself to one outcome or another. The hand, a dark splay on the paler field of her flesh, reminded her of the plump sea stars she'd seen in nature documentaries, bunching and spreading in slow, muscular spasms, and for a moment she was able to imagine that she was the sea floor and the hand's movement across her body was perfectly natural. But then Padre Diego began to murmur into her neck – *Te quiero, te quiero* – I want you – and the fantasy collapsed. His hand advanced to the edge of her shorts. Like the rest of him, it was huge, and she imagined his fingers as battering rams; she did not want them probing at her crotch. But it was too late, because he had begun tugging at her underwear, trying to move the flimsy fabric out of the way.

Lee wanted it to stop; even years later she was sure about this. But at that moment her thoughts were darting birds, and she couldn't gather the right words to make this happen. Hitting Padre Diego would be like beating her fists against a mountain, a useless exercise. Nor could she imagine climbing over him and walking out into the night. Where would she go? *Nada para hacer.*

She was paralyzed, anyhow. The vastness of the priest's transgression – his hand inside her underwear – transfixed her, like frogs falling from the sky. She thought about Father Pat touching her the way Padre Diego was touching her at that moment, and revulsion coursed down the backs of her legs like an electric charge. Revulsion and arousal, a sickening combination.

Padre Diego kept his hand on her knee during the entire drive back to Comalapa. Instead of taking her directly to Cristina and Paolo's, he pulled over onto a secluded road just outside of the town limits, turned off the engine, and groped her for 10 or 15 minutes. Lee thought about the dog while this was happening, felt its small, solid impact as a knot in her chest.

Soon after, Lee moved out of Cristina and Paolo's chicken shed and into a small room at the rectory. She had started

marketing the cooperative's coffee in Europe and needed to be
at the office early in the morning to place calls; at least, this was
the pretext for her move. Each night, Padre Diego would tap on
her door, and she would let him in. *I am doing this because I
want to,* she told herself. But the truth was, she had missed her
opportunity to opt out of the affair. Opting out meant thinking about what happened in the truck as an assault, and Lee
didn't like thinking about what happened in the truck at all;
how she had turned into something flat and inert, a landscape
upon which a calamity occurred. Besides, if she thought of it as
an assault, she would have to do something about it: inform the
police, or, at a minimum, pack up and go home. But nothing
waited for her at home; no grad program, no job, no partner,
no supportive group of friends. She'd screwed all that up. She'd
come to Chiapas for a hard reset, hoping to remake herself into
a tough and adventurous humanitarian. Someone who drank
mezcal and picked bodies out of mudslides. Someone bold and
desirable.

She began travelling with Padre Diego to conferences and
up into the *cafetales,* visiting remote communities where she
might as well have been an alien, and no one thought to question her association with the priest. Padre Diego often extended
these trips for a night or two, renting honeymoon suites in
motels on the outskirts of towns – once a room with a mirrored
ceiling that she squeezed her eyes shut against. Lee grew accus-
tomed to her revulsion. She figured it was the price of admis-
sion for the experiences she gained access to, which included
attending a secret meeting of insurrectionists and witnessing
the birth of a child. She was often treated as an honoured guest
on these occasions; offered a chair while others sat on the
ground or urged onto the back of a donkey up the steep paths
to the *cafetales.* Once, in the wretched hut of an old village

patriarch, she'd been presented with a hard-boiled egg while everyone else ate a poor meal of starchy tamales, and she'd had to choke it down despite loathing eggs. She was uneasy with this preferential treatment, but she didn't see what she could do about it. Padre Diego also gave her gifts: amber earrings, a Zapatista doll, and a colourful Mayan dress that looked wrong on her tall, pale body. Lee accepted these too, even though each gift further cemented their arrangement.

Lee suspected their relationship was an open secret in Comalapa but, if it was, few appeared to be scandalized by it. Paolo, perhaps, had begun treating her a little more coldly, but he had never liked her in the first place. Cristina seemed to accept the affair as an inevitability, as if it were perfectly normal for Lee to be sleeping with a Catholic priest. Almost everyone else in the town was poor and Mayan, and their inner thoughts were a mystery to her. Only Doña Lety made her disapproval known. She still served Lee at the counter of her bodega when Lee was in the neighbourhood, but she never again invited her into the courtyard to play with her granddaughters, nor did she volunteer Rabo to accompany Lee when she walked back to the rectory after dark. Lee took to carrying a stick to swing at the dogs that challenged her, and when she passed the *cantina* she kept her head down and walked quickly.

Three months after the accident, in the middle of December, Padre Diego announced that they were going back to Ocosingo. This time, after the meetings, he would take her to a resort near an archaeological site she had mentioned wanting to visit. He told her this with pride, as if he alone could grant her this experience. By now, Lee's Spanish was passable; after six weeks of struggling, a switch seemed to go off in her head. But she found she needed to say little around Padre Diego. He used up all the words, told her things he felt she needed to know, sang along with the radio, made jokes she understood poorly, and declared, over and over, his love for her. When he prodded her to make her own declarations, she would say, *Tengo hielo por sangre.* I have ice for blood. Padre Diego always laughed, as if she were joking.

Lee thought she would recognize the place where they struck the dog, but when they reached the ugly outskirts of Ocosingo she realized she had missed it. Of course, they had been travelling in the opposite direction at the time of the accident, and it had happened at night. Perhaps on the way back she would find the spot, although in truth, she wasn't sure why she wanted to. Did she think she could return to the moment before the accident and change its outcome? The portal to that time had sealed shut and vanished, leaving her on the wrong side of it.

The resort was built to resemble a Mayan palace, landscaped with bougainvillea, palm trees, and hibiscus, and garishly decorated for Christmas. Padre Diego removed his cross before he exited the truck and locked it in the glove compartment. Although nothing now marked him as a priest, their pairing was an odd one, and Lee felt people's eyes on them as they waited in line at reception.

He insisted on going to the pool right away. Lee tried not to look at his body, large and slick with sweat, clad in a Speedo-like swimsuit that would have been an object of derision back home. She masked her revulsion by splashing and skipping away from him in the pool, making a game of it, a technique she had perfected over the preceding weeks.

A lone woman and a group of three men lounged poolside. The men chatted in French while the woman read a book with a German title. The woman was blonde and perhaps a little prematurely weathered from too many hours in the sun. She and the three men glanced up occasionally at Lee and Padre Diego's antics in the pool, making Lee feel self-conscious and awkward, as if she were putting on a performance. Padre Diego's overt demonstrations of desire embarrassed her. She wished she could convey to her onlookers that her connection to the priest was temporary and unserious.

The woman and one of the men struck up a conversation in English, discussing their impressions of the ruins they had visited that morning. Lee drew nearer to listen in, so close she could smell the lotion on the woman's skin and see the fine, translucent hairs on her arms. Their familiar words were like raindrops on her parched mind, and she had to fight the urge to interject. How good it would feel to join in, she thought. Padre Diego, with his toddler's command of English, would be left out entirely.

They ate dinner in the hotel dining room. Padre Diego had been drinking steadily all afternoon; first beer, and now, because Lee requested it, wine. By the time their main courses arrived, they were on their second bottle and Padre Diego had begun to lean on the table, face slack and heavy-lidded. Lee had refused to have sex with him when they returned to their room after swimming, and the energy between them was strained. She had decided, in fact, never to have sex with him again. She hadn't yet informed Padre Diego of this development in their relationship, however. Instead, she told him she was going to spend a few weeks travelling around the Yucatan and Quintana Roo, a plan that had just come to her. Padre Diego's expression turned sour. He would drive her to the airport, he said, and meet her in Cancun as soon as he finished celebrating the Christmas Masses. Lee agreed, even though she had no intention of visiting Cancun, or meeting up with him, or ever returning to Comalapa.

Padre Diego passed out before the waiter returned to clear their plates. Lee tried to rouse him, prodding him roughly and hissing in his ear, but it was no use. Now that she had decided it was over between them, it was impossible for her to keep her revulsion at bay. She was astonished she had ever allowed this man to touch her – to lower his bulk on top of her, thrust his tongue into her mouth, and squeeze her ass as he came. *Se movió?* he would always ask when he finished. No. The Earth had not moved.

Finally, the waiter suggested that the Señor rest there awhile, and Lee gratefully left. She did not go back to the room, however, because she couldn't bear the thought of listening for the sound of Padre Diego's footsteps outside the door, his basso profundo muttering, his fumbling with the key. Instead, she walked across the torch-lit garden, sat at the poolside bar, and ordered a glass of wine she didn't need. The three French men and the German woman were at a small table nearby, laughing and smoking. Lee wanted to join them but could not summon the courage, so she pretended to be absorbed in a game on her phone. Finally, the men said goodnight and left the woman alone at the table, and Lee was emboldened to approach her and ask for a cigarette.

Her name was Jutta, or maybe Anja. She told Lee that she was a legal translator from Hamburg who had come to Chiapas to see the ruins and escape the dreary north German winter for a few weeks. Of course, she had noticed Lee, she said, and wondered about the man she was with.

For a moment, Lee wanted to tell her everything; about the dog, and what Padre Diego had done to her in the truck. About how she hadn't known what to do or where to go and how, as a result, she'd done nothing. But everything was knotted up in her mind and untangling it seemed impossible. So Lee sucked on her cigarette and told the woman the story she'd been telling herself, that the relationship was a wild and unconventional affair that had run its course. The woman's eyes widened when she learned that Padre Diego was a priest, making Lee feel bold and desirable. The torchlight sent shadows of fronds dancing over the woman's bare shoulders. Lee stubbed out her cigarette and asked for a second.

Voices filtered across the patio from the darkened restaurant; Padre Diego's and the waiter's. Quick, Lee said, grabbing the woman's hand. She pulled her across the stone patio, past the pool, and into a dark corner of the garden, drawing her down behind a screen of yucca and bougainvillea. They sat for a moment without speaking, submerged in the steady insect drone of night. Lee sensed that the woman did not want to be there – she'd had to pull a little harder than she expected – but her excitement at hiding from Padre Diego overpowered it, filling her chest like a balloon. She wasn't sure what to do next, though. Ask the woman for another cigarette? Or maybe she should do something crazy, like put her hand on the back of the woman's head and draw her in for a kiss. Lee leaned toward the woman, but the woman shifted away.

Listen, the woman said. You have no idea what you're doing.

The words landed like a slap, making heat rise in Lee's face. She thought about getting up and leaving, but nothing beyond the screen of bougainvillea felt safe.

If you need to sleep on my floor, you can. But that's all.

Lee squeezed her eyes shut. She tried to summon some cool and unbothered response to the woman but discovered she couldn't speak around the lump in her throat. Nor could she think properly. My mind is filled with garbage, she thought. Toxic, churning garbage. She was drowning in it. Yet there, in the middle of her defiled thoughts, she found the memory of Doña Lety's granddaughters: their weight on her lap, their clean, unfamiliar smell. The person she had been when she was with them.

The voices from the restaurant had now ceased, overtaken by the chirruping of the insects and the frogs. Padre Diego was probably asleep. Lee pictured him lying on his back, his massive face pointed at the ceiling, snoring. At least all of that was finished now.

Lee had been afraid that the woman would be gone when she opened her eyes, but she was still there, staring at her with a frankness that made Lee feel as if neither clothes nor even skin covered her.

I forget your name, Lee said, forcing herself to maintain eye contact. Could you tell it to me again?

Bruce Meyer

DRAGON BLOOD

"That's how those creatures sharpen their claws," the cobbler said.

The other men nodded. They looked to him as a source of knowledge. In fact, he knew nothing at all. His rank in the community was based on the fact he was the king of skittles and a champion at bowls.

What would happen if the monster reached the saffron fields and trampled the delicate flowers to the ground? The crocuses were just past their bloom. The stamens had been gathered. What would become of next year's harvest?

Those who thought they saw it described a large snake with eight legs. Did it breathe fire? Would it pounce on them and tear them to shreds? Some said there were no such things, that dragons were vanquished long ago. Saint George was real. He was the angel who guarded the nation. No one would craft a lie about that. But what if they had been real? Did they still lurk in chambers at the bottoms of lakes and terrify mankind as they had once done? What if the apparition was a dragon?

As the fog burned off, the hunters found evidence of scorched earth. Dragons breathe fire. They found the bones of three roasted sheep. If a dragon hungered for a lamb, why not a man? And there were markings on the trees nearby, scratches carved in the tree trunks. Each claw mark was filled with a red sticky paste.

"Blood of the lamb," the cobbler whispered. "As in the Bible. A plague is on our land."

The others nodded.

Aside from the fears of losing their livestock, the eight-legged creature awoke ancient horror. They could picture the beast trampling their precious walled field. The name of the town depended on that patch.

Saffron Walden. A field of crocuses.

What had awakened the beast of legend? Should they consult the *Book of Thel* or the *Book of Daniel*? Was this a portent of how the world would end? A dragon was a precursor of a land plagued with pestilence and sores. Where was the saint who would stand up against it? Who, among them, would be their Saint George? Were they the lambs being led to the slaughter?

—⟩⟨—

Admiral Qi dropped anchor off the eastern shore. Most days his ship was hidden by fog. It was springtime in this place of rain. Qi lowered his bamboo sails. The shift of the tide moved his ship in a circle. Though his vessel was named *Shining Sun on Waves*, he needed the fog to be his cloak.

He had fired on fishermen who came too close. They dropped their nets and rowed away.

He was desperate to replenish their food and fresh water. Their last landfall had been Be Zh u, not the near coast but the far other side where he witnessed people with dark skins shackled and loaded onto ships. He could do nothing. He was outgunned.

At the land of rain, Qi sent a landing party ashore. Han were not welcomed in the X waters. He knew their chance of survival was slim but he chose his second in command to lead the landing party. Zheng was the bravest among the ship's company. If they were to have any chance at success they would have to venture in disguise.

People, Zheng said, were afraid of two things: well-armed intruders who they would stand and fight, and creatures they would run from without a fight. It made good sense. Disguise would accomplish the latter. The landing party was instructed to move to the west, heading toward X where the sun always set. They were to mark their route by carving numbers in trees and each number would be inscribed with red ink. If they became lost they could retrace their steps by following their markings until they reached the sea.

But just as Zheng's men put ashore, Admiral Qi's ship came under fire. The attacking ship had a swan on its prow and was likely a warship that outgunned and outmanned *Sun Shining on Waves*. Rather than risk his ship and his crew, Qi withdrew into a fog and his shallow draught took him close to shore where the larger, deeper enemy could not follow.

Zheng ordered his landing party to don the disguise, a mask that was certain to frighten the pale ones.

"Ghosts always run from the bravery we wear," Zheng said. "We shall wear the dragon on our shoulders and in our hearts."

Qi had prepared for the voyage by commissioning a dragon so if, along the way, they encountered people who were friendly to the Han, they would entertain their hosts with a dragon dance.

To survive the dampness and the hardships of the voyage, the dragon would have to have leather for skin. It would be red, for courage and joy so even if *Sun Shining on Waves* vanished into a springtime fog, Zheng and his party would carry its strength on their shoulders and know it was never far from them. Qi's ship wore dragons on its sails.

"You, Zheng and your dragon men, are the bravest of the brave. You have come farther than any Han has travelled. We are in a dark place now, a land of constant rain and fog," said Qi. "But do not fear. We are a small force, and though outnumbered, you shall wear the skin of the dragon on your shoulders and the fire of its strength in your hearts."

Qi trusted the courage of his men. He believed all his sailors possessed courage even if they struggled to find it. He had risen in the ranks because he led by example. He instilled his sailors with clear-minded thinking to do their duty whatever obstacles they faced.

After defeating a fleet of pirates from Taohuagang laying siege to the fishing city of Ningbo, Admiral Qi was ordered to explore the X (western) ocean beyond which little was known of its realms. A scribe in the Palace of Eternal Water unrolled an ancient map and pointed with a stylus at the empty seas far beyond India.

The scribe said that this land was where the foreigners lived. Their ships were sturdy. When they came to trade among the Han they had endured great hardships and travelled tremendous distances. There was profit in their ventures.

The map depicted the outline of eastern Africa, but beyond that lay the sea which the ghosts called home. Qi was told that if the foreigners could brave such seas, a man of his courage would triumph over the waves. He was given a single ship, *Sun Shining on Waves*, and told to select the best men he could find for his crew.

Within months, having put the emptiness of the X ocean behind him, Qi turned his bow toward the b i (north) waters.

The sea before him was vast and friends would be difficult to find there.

At first, the waters were cold and stormy and grew even colder as they hugged the coast of what he knew was the far side of Fe Zh u, or what the Portuguese traders called Africa. The Han, though, had never ventured that far north. Why should they? When traders came to them there was little to be gained by following them home. Reason dictated that the Han should let the wealth of foreigners come to them. The seas were rough. Han ships that had ventured that far from home seldom returned. But the cold ocean suddenly became warmer as the current pushed them toward u Zh u, a land the outsiders called Europe. Then the winds died. *Sun Shining on Waves* was becalmed. The sun beat down upon the crew. The men grew thirsty.

The currents were the least of Qi's troubles. The weather in the year of Qi's voyage was unusual. Reports from everywhere Han ships sailed said that odd storms arose. The winds were not as anyone anticipated.

Though Qi had no way of knowing it, meteorological accounts of the spring of 1686 describe the season as one of the rainiest on record for England. When the horizon was not curtained in rain a veil of fog overran the waters. Qi's men collected rainwater as it fell.

1686 was also the year the fields of eastern England turned to mud. Nothing grew. Those who augured the skies said that mischief was afoot in the world.

In the constant downpour, unable to find shelter, hungry, foraging for what they could find or take from the fields, the men under Zheng's command soon lost their way. Their markings in Dragon Red, the numbers they painted so carefully as they began their trek inland, did not dry. Dragon Red, a hue of

ink produced in India and favoured by scribes in the vast
bureaucracy of the Middle Kingdom would only set in a warm
room. Outdoors, painted on trees, the numbers ran in the rain
or became a sticky ooze in each wound Zheng's men carved in
the trees to mark their nocturnal march inland in search of pro-
visions. And when Zheng tried to find the sun, he found its
light glowing in all directions behind the low, grey clouds.

━╱╲━

The cobbler, whose name was Isaiah Corbett, boasted he had
killed the dragon. He insisted to all who would listen at his
shop door that the same skilled eye that had made him a champion at bowls and skittles enabled him to slay the dreaded beast.
At first, the townsfolk of Saffron Walden were grateful and
acclaimed Corbett as their very own Saint George, though he
would have had an even better claim to fame if he had stepped
forward with a pike and in the manner of the legendary saint
who had slain the beast with his lance and brought the dragon's
head with him to the village as a trophy from his combat. If he
didn't use a lance, one woman questioned, how did Corbett kill
the monster? Corbett refused to answer.

The rain began to let up. The fields began to dry though it
was almost too late in the season for them to plant a decent
crop. The crocuses were drowned. The townsfolk said, "Take us
to the body of the beast. We want to see it for ourselves. We can
sell parts of it to offset our losses with the saffron."

Corbett said it was dark, early morning, when the combat
in the forest had taken place. The air was thick with fog, so
thick he could not recall the precise location in which he felled
the dragon. He thought he had used a pike but had left it in the
belly of the beast. Why had he abandoned the other men? Was

he mad or simply foolish? Alone, he made the perfect target for the dragon. He had been a fool. And could the word of a fool be trusted? An old woman, the widow of a baker who had died the previous winter, confronted Corbett to provide proof that his story was true.

"If you were there once you can go there again and we will follow you."

Then someone raised the possibility that the dragon might not be dead at all. It might be merely wounded, and "a wounded dragon would be looking to avenge its suffering even if the gashes Corbett inflicted would eventually be mortal wounds."

Corbett had no choice but to lead a tour into the sycamore copse and produce the body. One man said he thought he smell rotting flesh and noted, "Dragons leave a terrible stink." They found nothing and while a dragon could not be captured it did feed enough fear to make a good tale. The creature soon became a topic of conversation.

The story of the Dragon of Saffron Walden spread to London. Men of reason scoffed at the idea but the curious were drawn to the spectacle a dead dragon might present. Roads to the village were crammed with the curious. Merchants in the town raised their prices and evolved the ethos of a carnival.

Among those who came up from London to say they had been there when the dragon, dead or alive, was revealed to the world, was the painter Godfrey Kneller, a rising portrait artist who, although talented, was still seeking his first note-worthy commission. Kneller knew he had to capture the spirit of someone who possessed a future – a man of science – and despite rebuffs he pursued a young mathematician who had already explained why the Earth attracted falling bodies.

Kneller knew the mathematician was interested in two things: numbers and colours. Perhaps the number of scales on a dragon's back, a meeting of zoology and arithmetic in a pattern that presented or defied the Fibonacci sequence, would interest Kneller's sitter. Perhaps even a scale from the monster's back, iridescent as a hummingbird's feathers, would incite the man of science's curiosity enough to arrange a sitting for a portrait. And if the dragon was real, the new science of zoology would be altered with relics from ancient folklore.

Early on the morning of June 5, as the sun rose in a low mist on the fields and the dewed tufts of grass sparkled like fairy crowns, a tour of a hundred souls with Corbett at the front walked toward the woods. Kneller, along with many others in the procession, stopped at the edge of the forest.

Corbett explained that if his memory served him, he and his group of yeomen had ventured into the heart of the mystery at that point, armed only with a flintlock pistol and the weapons one might either take from a barn or whittle to a fine point the night before their search for the dreaded dragon. Some on the tour were bored by the commentary. Others were eager to see the dragon for themselves and pressed ahead. They were warned not to stray too far from the procession in case the beast was merely wounded and lurked behind the trees for an opportunity to avenge the wrongs done to it.

"You do not know what perils await you," Corbett called after them in a flare of showmanship.

Within a hundred yards of the clearing, the crowd had spread out, most looking for souvenirs of the fearsome creature. One little girl shouted that she had found a tooth from the monster, but on close inspection, it was only the tusk of a wild boar. A woman was certain she had found a scale clutching the roots of a tree but the object was nothing more than a toadstool. No matter how hard the crowd searched, not a trace of the dragon was found. Most began to wander back to the village, angry that they had wasted their time searching for a figment of someone's imagination.

Kneller, however, was one of the last to leave the forest. He had gotten a twig inside his shoe and leaned against a tree to empty it. When he pulled his hand from the trunk of a sycamore, the eastern side of the tree was carved with a strange set of parallel sticks, one short one above a longer one, both slightly slanted. They had been carved not merely as a lover's knot or even a symbol or a vagrant's warning but as a form of writing. The lines had been painted with a gummy red substance that would not wipe clean from Kneller's palm.

He stared at it. He was certain he had seen the odd configuration of lines before. He walked due east to the other side of the forest and found another carving on another sycamore – this one composed of three horizontal lines. These were no mere dragon scratches. They were meant to mark someone's way, signposts for a path out of the woods, made perhaps by a person who was lost and left as markers so they would not retrace their steps and wander in circles. He took out his artist's sketch pad and pressed his palm to the paper and in doing so printed the image on the page.

On his return to London two days later, he consulted a sea captain who had made numerous voyages to the Far East for cargoes of blue and white porcelain he sold to wealthy London merchant families as decorations for their houses. The sea captain stood in the light of his greeting room window and examined the page from Kneller's notebook.

"These, sir, are Chinese numbers. I know them from pottery merchants in the East. They would show me their account books to make me believe they were doing an honest business.

Little did they know, I had learned to read their columns of figures. I did very well on those voyages. This is the number three."

The Van Gelder paper in the notebook held the dark red marks. Kneller sent one sample, the number two, to Isaac Newton, requesting that the natural philosopher study the odd deep red for the virtues and character of its hue. The mathematician agreed to admit him for an audience.

Newton was fascinated by the colour. The red was not bright but a deeper tone, more like dried blood than any red he had seen in artists' studios. But the semblance of blood about it made Newton uneasy. Who on earth would favour such a tone? Red was meant to be a lively colour, the shade of vitality but not morbidity, and this red was beyond any red his experiments with colour had revealed to him. The red on the Van Gelder paper was troubling, mysterious, and full of secrets. It was not a red to be entertained. He and Kneller agreed that they could live without it. It was, indeed, the colour of dried blood. The red was splattered on a plank of driftwood and when it dried it had unnerved Kneller because the dragon blood was not from a dragon. It was the blood of murdered men.

Kneller admitted he had witnessed the dragon's slaughter on the beach near Maldon. There had, indeed, been a dragon. It contained unarmed men. Their death had been a spectacle. The unarmed men emerged from the body of the mythic serpent and were felled by musket balls as they tried to flee. Were they pirates? He could not say for sure; but the image of their pain, their twisted faces, and their hands reaching out to a ship offshore haunted his nightmares. The images would not let him be.

"Those men were slaughtered without trial or question. They were shot on the beach and in the shallows by a patrol of the King's Own Men.

"Tell no one," Newton said. "Do not speak of what you witnessed. What you saw was the felling of the last of all the English dragons. What you saw was Saint George in combat. And if you speak of it, no one will believe you. No one believes in dragons anymore."

Newton leaned forward toward the fire in his hearth, holding the sample of the colour in his hand. "May I?" he asked, and Kneller nodded. "You saw nothing," he said, wiping his hand on the front of his waistcoat. "For your own future, and perhaps for mine, the colour you found does not exist."

In the first portrait Kneller painted of the author, *Philosophæ Naturalis Principia Mathematica*, there is not a single brushstroke of red, an omission both men agreed to in advance of the sitting.

―✦―

The sun was not an ally for an Admiral attempting to hide his ship. *Sun on Shining Waves* was unlike any vessel on the seas to the X of u Zh u, the North Atlantic. Its square bamboo sails were designed to capture the maximum amount of wind, but the hull of the ship was designed for stability in typhoons and rough seas and not for speed. Qi knew that if he took *Sun Shining on Waves* into the shallows, he might come under cannon fire from the land and if he sailed into deeper waters, the ships from the land of rain would surround him and outgun him and show him no mercy.

On the fifth of June, Qi decided he would draw the enemy to him. Everything he knew about warfare advised him to taunt but not to touch his opponent's superior forces. His knowledge of the complexities of u Zh u told him Europe was not a unified place, not like Zh ngguó where the entire world of the Han was governed by the power of Heaven. He decided to draw the enemy out and then do the unexpected: circle back and retrieve Zheng's landing party – if they were still alive – and then sail Nàn (south) toward another kingdom. If he was lucky he could create a confrontation between enemies while *Sun Shining on Waves* slipped away.

But the boat used by Zheng to put ashore had been discovered in the dunes where his men had buried it. News reached London that Chinese characters had been read on trees near Saffron Walden, and a dory that fit no known description of a fishing boat had been located on a beach near Maldon. The Royal Navy's *Swan* had exchanged fire with a vessel that could only be described as Asiatic in origin. The outsiders had to be repulsed. Trade with China would remain at arm's length.

—⁄ι⳽—

Zheng and the landing party made it to the beach where they had put ashore a month before. They had failed to acquire the Admiral's supplies and had spent their return trek to the coast running for their lives, pursued by men in red. He would feel shame to return empty-handed. He prayed that *Sun on Shining Waves* was still safe and had not been sunk by the strange people of the land of rain. He would return the Admiral's dragon intact in the hope that somewhere they would be greeted with kindness.

As Zheng's party emerged from the low trees that led to the dune where they had buried their dory, he realized the spot had been disturbed. Behind them, and well within hearing, a column of men in red coats and pointed black hats was approaching from behind. It would be foolish for anyone to search for the dory. Zheng had to assume it was gone.

He was about to despair his men would be caught between the sea and the soldiers when *Sun Shining on Waves* appeared around a headland and weighed anchor a hundred yards off-shore.

One of the red soldiers, a man with a sword, was yelling commands at Zheng and his men. Granted, Zheng's men had lived off the land. They had stolen sheep to survive. What was a crime in Zh ngguó was most likely a crime in the land of rain.

In one final act of defiance, he ordered his men to become the dragon. They would not fight. They would dance for their enemy. They would snake their way across the beach and from there those who could swim would make their way to their ship. If they died they would die with the courage of dragons. They would rear their heads and beat their drum. The idea seemed absurd to Zheng but, exhausted and haggard along with his men, he felt he had no other option.

The dragon leaped from the undergrowth.

It spun, snarled, and roared red glory, turning and shaking its head at the soldiers, some of whom were standing, others kneeling, as they raised their muskets and aimed at the creature.

Zheng's men danced to the edge of the waves when the man with the sword shouted a single word and musket balls tore through the dragon's flesh. Three men dropped. But the dance continued. The dragon danced into the water, its tail rising and falling in the arms of those who held it and shook its head.

Another volley.

Zheng saw two more of his men collapse. He felt a firebolt tear through his shoulder. He let go of the head and saw it for an instant bobbing beside him in the waves. The water turned red with dragon blood.

He could see his ship drawing closer as a ball struck him in the back of his head and this dreams of Zh ngguó and the dragon-toothed shores where his brothers were sitting and mending their nets faded to a dream of eternal night.

Admiral Qi ordered his men to make full sail as three ships rounded the headland, cutting off their passage to the open sea. Desperate not to be defeated easily now that victory or escape was hopeless, Qi ordered his pilot to steer a new course.

"Aim for the biggest ship!" he shouted. "Prepare yourselves to fight to the end."

He sent five men below to spill every ounce of oil they were carrying and set *Sun Shining on Waves* ablaze.

"Prepare the barrels of gun powder forward!"

They would ram the enemy and fight to the death.

The bow of Qi's ship was about to collide with the side of the largest enemy ship when its heavy guns breathed a shout of fire. Those who survived the cannonade did not survive the combat. *Sun Shining on Waves* exploded, far enough from the enemy to do no damage. The bamboo sail, burning, collapsed, and the hull of Qi's ship hissed in the waves, leaving shards of tiny floating flames that shone like broken fragments of sun.

The battle was of little consequence. A note about the skirmish was slipped into the back of a logbook at the Greenwich Office of Admiralty Records, but at some point in time, the note had disappeared. The three British ships, with no men lost, sailed south toward the mouth of the Thames where the largest ship, the *Royal Venture*, was quickly repainted to erase signs of combat.

No one in diplomatic circles in London was any the wiser for what had happened, and ships from England plied their trade routes to China round the Cape of Good Hope. They came first for spices and pottery, then for the tea, the most precious commodity the Empire had known.

The captain of the *Royal Venture* was summoned to St. James Palace by the newly crowned monarch, James II. As a token of thanks and a purchase of silence, the captain was given a small blue and white jar containing a new drink that was popular at court. The sweet-smelling, dried green leaves became a beverage when added to hot water. The jar that held them was blue and white porcelain and painted with dragons on both sides.

When writing an official explanation of the disappearance of Admiral Qi and his ship, *Sun Shining on Waves*, along with its entire crew, a scribe in the Palace of Eternal Waters rose early one morning and bathed his body in a bowl of cold water. He wanted to be sure the narrative he would write would be about more than a ship being lost, sucked under by a wave in the vast empty X between Zhōngguó and FēZhōu. The Admiral, whom he noted he had met twice, was an elegant man who had a natural air of seamanship and gallantry about him.

The scribe began by grinding red berries into a paste that had been brought from India by Buddhist monks. The paste was cut with liquified pig's fat and made fluid with some drops of expensive plum wine. He stared into the bowl of red ink, saw his reflection, and set to work.

The aroma of the plum wine made him wonder how dragon blood ink might taste but the fact the other scribes never consumed it made him think twice about putting some on his tongue. He had heard stories of monks far away, who lived a long time ago on an island in the cold. Their lives were surrounded by the northern sea where they copied their texts onto scraped skins of deer. If anything, the story was something to scoff at, yet there was a sense of wonder to it. It was said the monks shovelled the words from their mouths and to do so wetted the tips of their brushes between their lips to make the ink more pliable. It sounded ridiculous.

For a moment, though, he considered the puzzling idea of writing on deerskin and thought it a waste of such a beautiful animal, and tried to imagine the taste of deer meat, though most dishes that came to the Palace of Eternal Waters were served first to the Emperor or his chief appointee. What the men above him did not want was passed down the chain of command, and one time he was lucky to have been given a dish of venison cured in cinnamon and spiced with cloves. It was delicious on top of his ration of rice. He wished he could have asked for more but a man in his position was not permitted to ask for anything other than what he was given.

On paper, better than deerskin for the ink, the story of the bravery of Admiral Qi needed no embellishment and was given the reverence the Admiral deserved. Instead of wasting the ink on his tongue, he dipped his brush in the deep red liquid and began to write of an endless voyage to where the sun never set, even on rainy days when the rain would not stop. And he was pleased as the fine brush tip wrote the characters. The Admiral would be honoured if he was there to see it.

Dragon Blood was the ink reserved for the most important stories. When it dried, the scribe rolled up the lengths of paper, some illustrated with pictures of *Sun Shining on Waves*, and placed them in a bamboo tube covered in fine gold leaf. He set it on a shelf in the Palace of Eternal Waters where he was sure it would remain forever, and its deep, perfect red, the colour of honour, would glow brighter than the drowning sun after it sets in the western waves.

Layne Coleman

TONY NAPPO RUINED MY LIFE

My face is okay, but where I really shine is with my wild fanny. It's next level.

I was making a sort of living as a sports broadcaster on talk radio but I thought I'd go for being an actress. I had a decent voice. It was a growl more than a voice. It was an invitation – come play. When I whispered I could make cats follow me.

I couldn't afford acting school. So I worked a day shift which wasn't as good money. I took classes at night. My life was just getting started.

I studied with a guy who taught classes from a shit place above a garage. Whenever it was my time to work he'd wink at me. I don't think he ever learned my name.

He'd say things like, "When you sit in a chair, just sit down. Don't act sitting in the chair. Take a seat. Don't think about it. Make sure you're thinking about something else."

"What should I be thinking?"

"Think about your next move. Ask yourself, 'Why am I in this room? How am I'm going to get whatever it is I came here to find?'"

I'd look confused, which I was. I knew about hockey but not sitting in chairs.

He'd say, "You're here to find love. That's why we take the first step into any room. All the boring stuff you have to do in this life is just looking for sex. Or love, same thing." He was walking back and forth as he talked. "I have a seven-month-old son. I feed him bananas every morning. He cries after every mouthful. He can't stand the time between bites. Life is the stuff that happens between bites. Love is the bite. Make sure you bring only the bite onto the stage."

Maybe I had what it takes to be an actor? I was needy. I knew how to relax in a make-believe world.

I got my picture taken for my headshot. My back to the camera, I looked over my shoulder at the lens. The photographer said that wasn't the normal way you did these kind of shots. Turned out it worked. I had an agent in no time, and when she sent my picture out I got an audition first thing. It was only a general audition. Which means you're not really doing anything more than meeting the person who might give you a job.

In this case, it was a guy about 30 years old who was taking over a theatre in Saskatoon that was just getting going. He was doing two days of generals. By the time I got to him he looked nearly blind. He'd seen somebody every five minutes and he was halfway through the second day. We were in another shit room somewhere. I was beginning to get the impression that a lot of acting was done in shit rooms.

He didn't get up from the couch to greet me. His smile was quite insincere by this point. He looked like he was in over his head. I'm a sucker for lost boys.

I didn't waste any time. I took up my position in front of him. I'd prepared a monologue and practiced in front of the bathroom mirror. I always said it the same way and I was boring myself to tears. I made a fateful decision. I showed him my best feature instead. I stood there for a long time. Giving him a good look. If I had five minutes that's how long I'd take. He never said a word. Neither did I. When I turned around his eyes were running water. He blinked and said, "That was great. Do you do any Shakespeare?"

I didn't. That was fine with him 'cause he didn't either. He thought he might have a part for me. He liked my voice. It didn't seem like I gave a shit and that's what he was looking for. The character he was thinking about was a lap dancer.

Why did that feel like an insult? "I'm not much of a dancer. My dad was not a fan of the pole. He raised me to be suspicious of poles and ladders. Is this one of those plays where the dancer meets a decent man like a theatre director and ends up starring in a play about herself?"

He laughed and I liked his laugh, it wasn't a defence mechanism. I felt welcome to have an opinion.

"You're right, that's pretty much what it is."

I took a wild stab at sincerity. "I'm sure it's well written."

He looked somewhere above my head. It was a small, claustrophobic room with a low ceiling so there wasn't much space for him to avoid my eyes. Speaking to the invisible fourth wall he said, "She came to Canada, lied about her age to cross the border. She was running from Jerry Falwell's church. A church dodger from America. She worked a lunch club near Bay Street. Her mother phoned from the church, begged her to reconsider her life choices. Her mom told her Jesus stopped loving her today. I saw the show after that phone call. It was transcendent."

"May I ask how many women were at that performance?"

"I don't recall seeing any."

"The only woman there just happened to be on the stage then?"

"It was a small demographic."

I asked him why he thought I'd be good for that part.

My voice made him feel like he was riding in a pink Cadillac going straight to hell. That's what he was looking for. He was willing to commit to me right then.

I liked this acting thing more than ever.

He was flying back to Saskatoon tomorrow. He'd phone me with the details. I stood there wondering what my next move should be. Did he expect me to fuck him right there, to say thank you? Or was that something that would come later?

"I'm interested," he said, "in what you think of my play idea. I mean, I know you haven't read it or anything, but on first blush, what's your impulse?"

He leaned back a little on his couch like he was expecting a blow from my fist. He looked paler than when I entered the room. I knew the power had shifted to my side. I know what is expected at a moment like this. But for some reason I liked the guy. I went with the truth.

"A lot of people see women in a victim light. A young girl gets herself all turned around and makes some dough selling her assets like they were jars of jam or pies at a bake sale. I've entertained the idea of it myself. But what generally happens – it makes people uncomfortable. It's not a turn-on. What is freely given is not that interesting. Take me, for example: I'm in sports. I'm a sports broadcaster. I work a radio show. What I'm selling is not anything that's dear to me. I was raised by a dad who did nothing but watch sports on television and he talked back to the screen. He made me laugh. That's what made me interested in him and sports. I picked up a lot of information from him that I was able to translate into a paycheque. It's a man's world, but women live here too and have for a long time. We aren't just a pussy looking for a dick. But guys have a hard time picking that up. I'm pretty sure your story carries that kind of message. Let's say you changed your story to mine. It's the story of a woman where she's not intended to be, in sports. That's the best way to get somebody's attention. You wonder if someone is going to kill the girl for daring to open her mouth without a dick between her legs. There's a big difference between selling men something they already believe. Lap dancers are selling the fiction that if a man is married he just becomes hotter. If you're selling what everyone believes, except for women, you won't get far. You got to appeal to the women. They recognize dicks talking to other dicks. It's boring."

I knew it was a risk. I could tell he thought he was taking a big chance with his play. He was pale as a bar of soap, but his eyes had some fire. He asked me if I could take a break from my job and come to Saskatchewan and work on a new idea. One about a daughter who learns sports from her dad. It sounded like a Christmas show to him. He wanted to make a big splash with his first show and this felt like a winner.

I jumped with both feet. "When do we start?"

~/\~

We were drunk before we started drinking. The guy had euphoria coming out of his ears. You could feel his lust like a blast furnace. He was clearly a hundred-yard dash man. That's okay with me. You fuck against the wall or in the toilet stall and then you can get back to drinking again. You don't need to spend all that time at his apartment pretending to enjoy his Spotify list, or in some shitty hotel room painted in loneliness. I don't feel as cheap fucking a guy in a bathroom as I do in a hotel. Hotels take all the fun out of sex. You have to be serious if you spend two hundred bucks for a room. You got to make it worthwhile for the person who's paying. It's not nice. I'd rather stumble around in an alley and improvise. I want to feel a person and see them at their worst. I don't want to lay around in a bathrobe talking about what restaurant we should eat at. I want sex to be like a car accident. Like you just discovered sex this very minute, and isn't it a big wallop of nasty doing?

He asked me what was my secret. He kept checking his cell phone.

I gave him a little taste of Dad. "Dad was pure Jazz. He sat on this ratty couch with one of the last turn-the-knob televisions in existence. He loved to perform for me. I was his audience of one. I was the last person on earth as far as he was concerned. We definitely lived on a desert island. I was his captive child. He was my dad. He'd made me from nothing. With a lot of help from you know who. She who was no longer there. My Lady of Immaculate Absence. Yes, she was dead, but that's no excuse."

The director instinctively reached for his cell phone. Red flag.

"Dad's pyjamas were him. As soon as he came home at the end of the day, he couldn't get into them fast enough. He looked like a badly wrapped Christmas present in them. But he was the only present under the tree and that present had my name on it."

I had a notion that the director was one of those impressed by metaphors. "My dad was bored by the melody. He worked from chord structure. The melody was improvised. It changed. Dad wanted to know himself, but that was impossible 'cause he was always changing. He lived between chaos and beauty. It's a great place to be, but it's also tragic. Dad wanted to get lost in the music. But instead of music it was the Leafs. He thought the Leafs were life. He said life was so much more terrible than anything you could imagine. The Leafs were my dad's toolkit. He sat on the couch with the shitty waterfall painting above his head and had a deep conversation with the Leafs. Was my dad a loser talking to losers? Once, after throwing a yogurt container at the television, he shouted: 'Pick up your guys on the way back. Don't wait for 'em to get sorted in hell. This is Canada. We play hockey. I promise you there's no hitting in heaven. Only singing. In heaven you have to find your note. On earth you have to pick up your guy in the neutral zone. No fucking the dog, no free lunch for the superstars. Everybody has to earn their keep.'"

The director drummed his fingers on his leg. "Okay," he said. "Give me more."

I made the director order another round of drinks. Maybe if he was gripping two glasses he'd put down his phone. The drinks arrived and he did something that I liked. He tipped the waitress 40 per cent. Nothing impresses me more than a man who tips. It means he's trying to get my attention. I stood for a second or two and turned around. Just to give him another quick look. It was carrot time. I reward my hostages for good behaviour. Besides, I like to stand up when I'm auditioning.

"Okay. Sports rant. Hockey player interviews are dull. It's something they're taught. Be positive. Never give the other guy a chance to get mad at you, he'll cream you. Calm the waters. Say the obvious. Paint inside the borders, here's the thing, I want truth. I want to hear a player say for once, 'The guy kneed me in the nuts. He's gonna pay.' Write it down. You might forget. Fuck the neutral zone, puck possession is the way into my pants. Did I say pants? I meant heart. Always be on the O."

The director leaned back and laughed. He laughed so hard he had to take another drink. Boys love it when you do these little Freudian slips. That's why they are an important part of my arsenal. I wagged my finger in his face.

"If you fuck the dog in your own end don't come crawling to me whining. Run the weed. Those kilos won't get into the back of the truck by themselves. The product you're selling is winning."

Whee, this is fun. Every joke is landing. I feel like I'm tickling the guy. He's as jolly as Jell-O. I move my face closer. Like I'm warning him about something he should know.

"My dad said when you go over the top there are at least four thousand ways you can die. There's only one way you're going to live. Luck. You have to please luck. Luck be a lady. But luck is a lady who doesn't text you back. When men invented a God it was because they wanted to appeal to a higher power than luck. Luck does not bargain. Luck does not sacrifice their son for Dog Fucking in their own end. Don't be sending LUCK no dick pictures." I stamped my feet for emphasis. This girl can act. Bang bang bang on the table with the hands. He likes that. He grabs my drink so I can't spill it. For a second I touch his hand and hold it there. Here's where I made a tasty little decision with my blocking. I sat down for emphasis. I could hear my acting teacher tell me that I was making good artistic choices. I used my hands maybe a little too much? I give myself a mental note to strip my shit down. Simplify. It was time to involve his intellect. I asked questions like I was some motherfucker from France.

"Great hockey players don't wait for the play to develop. You have to live in a land before knowledge. Hockey is panic. It's a process of continually losing your temper. The game manages this by allowing for certain acceptable levels of violence. You ever meet Wayne Gretzky?"

I couldn't believe it. He nodded he didn't know Gretzky. I spoke kind of distracted. I was changing it up. I wanted him to think I was having far-off thoughts. Maybe about another boy I knew and would call later?

"You don't get smart by shooting a puck against the wall in your backyard for your whole childhood. But Gretzky was pre-knowledge. He lived in a universe beyond luck. Before luck could find him. He didn't think. He was 100 per cent puck possession, rarely seen in his own end. His natural habitat was around the opposition's net." It was time to wrap it up. I gave him my regular sign off, cue the commercial.

The director was disappointed it was over. He took another sip. He stood and applauded. I bowed and for extra I gave him a little cheek to kiss. It was red carpet time. I heeded my gut. It was time to ask him about himself. Let him share the mic. I went back to the bench, my back against the wall so I could see the door and my director at the same time. I was about ready to take the man into the alley. I closed my eyes for a second like a woman dreaming. In a low and hoarse voice, then, "Tell me about you. What's Saskatoon like? What's your vision for the theatre?"

Vision is not something you want to throw around with arts types. They go on a little too much. Like they're writing a grant application. But I was genuinely interested.

The director took a long drink. "Saskatoon has a river running through it. Most eastern Canadians think it's pretty. I won't tell you about the sky. They have Wi-Fi. You can get pizza 24/7. The theatre is a building an uncle lets me use. It's in the round. Sometimes actors don't like having the audience on all four sides. I tell them it's like watching a film in 3D and that usually wins them over. I'm a fan of theatre in small rooms. Theatre In Small Rooms would be the vision."

I liked it when he talked theatre. I could tell that we would have a good post-coital life if it came to that.

The director said, "You're wearing Blundstones. Everybody wears them in the 'Toon. When you leave a party you'll never be able to find your shoes at the door. Saskatoon likes to fund buildings but nothing to put in them. Art is something you look at when you're on holidays in Europe. The audiences are good, though. I'm like a missionary out there. I look for converts. I can't leave the place."

I was feeling depressed. I wasn't feeling like it anymore. I didn't care about my drink. I didn't care about anything. My shit had gone listless. I was either going home or out to the alley. I didn't care which right now. I drank the rest of my glass. That was a sure sign I was going somewhere. "My dad would sit in the dark with his desires. He'd refuse to turn the lights on until the sun had completely disappeared. I hear people talk about appropriate and inappropriate. They're lucky. Some people don't have a gram of appropriate in them." Maybe I was fighting back tears. Should I stop drinking?

"Dad taught me forgiveness. Forgive the weak for they are always fighting. Anyone who fights loses. My dad called it, 'Long ago and far away in a land before cell phones, women would flirt with ya. Life was often boring and you couldn't distract yourself unless you flirted.' Naturally men got more attention. Boredom worked in men's favour. Not these days. With a cell phone a woman has other options. When a woman gets bored, everybody gets bored.'"

The director looked at the door. His eyes were sad, but still alive. "What happened to your dad?"

"He died."

I got up from the table and went outside. The director didn't follow. He looked at his cell phone. He had to read a post from some actor named Tony Nappo. Alone I go to the back alley, I was ready to give up the theatre. Who the fuck is Tony Nappo, and why was he ruining my life? Some over-sharing Dog Fucker in his own zone? He was standing between me and my full audition.

Well, look who's bringing up the rear? The director. And without his cell phone. Turning point: Actress discovered in alley rockets to stardom. It's so easy for a lady to lose her virtue in pursuit of her goals. I have to be stern. I review my riot act. No blow jobs. Hand jobs are like doing the dishes. Which leaves only kissing. What would my agent say?

"Make sure the guy is good for what he says. Otherwise you're just having sex."

That would be pathetic. What's my motivation? I'll ask my director. I grab him and swing him with mock violence against the wall. I say, "Imagine if we were in slo-mo."

The director has good limb control and stopgaps like a strobe light flashing off and on. He tells a story of a man powerless to protect himself. He screams NO. His body screams YES.

Who do you believe? The face, or the body? It's such a turn-on not knowing which one is telling the truth. There's no time or resources to poll the audience. This is strictly pin the tail on the donkey. But who is the donkey? I put my mouth close enough to be almost inside his ear. I can taste the baby he once was. I've hit a rich vein in the mine. The loins do not lie, but neither do they know what's happening on the perimeter. I was losing the big picture. "Make sure you're protecting the goalie." I whisper to the director. My voice is the sound of paper burning. "Who's your goalie?" My voice is also a garden snake. It stings and paralyzes, then kills.

His mouth opens, there's no sound. He's speaking in tongues. The director is host to a demon. I can see he's ashamed and I want to reward him for that shame. I put my broad lips close to his mouth. It's an exploratory measure. I want his people to coax my tongue into his mouth. It's a yes. All hell breaks loose. It's like Value Village. There's no more red lights. All my power as a co-creator just went out the window. I tell him with my hips that I want him to sign a rider. He loses the slo-mo and I stab him with my perfect V. He hurts so good. The dick says, "I'll sign anything." Saskatoon gets the win.

-⁄ı⋅-

The first thing you notice when you fly into Saskatoon is the number of ex-girlfriends your director has floating around the scene. That cools my jets. I have to navigate around in a big coat and meet the "community" as my director calls them.

Virginia is one of those passive aggressive exes. The kind that is marinated in bitterness and rejection. When you meet exes you think the same will not happen to you. Straight off she said it was surprising that the director had not cast locally. "There are plenty of super-talented women who could do your role."

I seriously doubt it, hasn't been written yet. There's a lot of hate for people from Toronto. I don't know what we did to deserve it.

The director says it has something to do with the freight rates of the CPR. We made farmers pay to ship their grain east. And they paid again when the east sent back the tractors and the plows. That didn't seem fair. "I'll assume all the women I meet have done you, and I'll apologize for the shipping rates."

The director said he'd ended it with Virginia because he didn't like her last performance. There was no going back after you saw a girlfriend acting badly on stage. Bad art is a buzz killer.

It didn't fill me with confidence as a woman, or as an actor. I was definitely at zero when I stood on the stage and looked out at the director sitting with the stage manager beside him. The stage manager was beautiful. She had red hair and this kind of androgynous thing she was working on. She wore boy clothing and a big Canadian beer toque. The director introduced her as his right arm. His lieutenant. He was helpless without her.

"If she's that good maybe she wants to replace me?"

He said the best way to proceed would be to enact all the things I was most ashamed of – those were the stories that usually prove to be the funniest.

"Well, at least we won't run out of material that way."

The stage manager laughed. It's easy to like someone who laughs at your jokes.

Let me see what makes me most ashamed. It's a long file. Shame has a long memory. "How about the time I interviewed the Rookie of the Year? We met in a bad Tex-Mex cafe on Yonge Street. The nachos were cardboard and they had some kind of cheese substitute on them. The room was set down below the street level. We had a table by the window with an unusual view of everybody on the sidewalk. By that I mean, you could look up a girl's skirt. I don't know what came over me. I really don't. I was lucky to get the interview and I guess I was nervous. The guy was cute and he was from the Peace River region. He hadn't been in a big city for very long. He was awkward with girls and I asked him how long he'd spent in the company of boys in dressing rooms. There's a strange dynamic between the interviewer and the interviewee. Who's more important? The storyteller or the Vic? This experience taught me that sex is about a power dynamic and so is journalism. The rookie says he's probably been in the company of mostly boys his whole life. I ask him what guys talk about on the bus when they're kids going to those shithole towns all across the country. They mostly talked about normal stuff. Girls. Who was doing what to whom. They listened to hip hop. If somebody farted that was a big deal. Everybody would move away from the offender. You got to know who the farters were and you wouldn't sit near them on the bus. I liked this guy. He was giving me gold. I'd been with him for at least five minutes and he hadn't mentioned how important it was for the team to win. How he just wanted to contribute. Maybe that was coming. Then a girl walked by us, one of those drop-dead gorgeous rich girls who went to the best private schools. She was wearing a thousand-dollar backpack and the wind blew the skirt and she tried to hold it down. She looked at the rookie of the year. She was surprised, so was the rookie. She had perfect teeth. She recognized the rookie and radiated a full beam smile. Then bee-lined out of our lives. The rookie glowed and stared at his nachos. Looked at me like he was an angel speaking God's truth. 'I'd crawl across 50 feet of cut glass and through a mile of 10-inch pipe to suck the cock of the last man who fucked her.'"

The red head laughed and dropped her coffee. The director asked me why the shame?

"I haven't finished telling the story. I was jealous of the girl. I'm ashamed of that. I thought – here we have a tough guy. A superstar and he would suck a man's dick in order to be with that particular woman. It seems preposterous to me now. I mean, he was making a joke. I whiffed on the metaphor. I said, 'I'll do all the dick sucking at this table, thank you very much.' The lines between good journalism and bad sex had blurred.

"Very unprofessional. I know you won't believe me, but I was seeking a better story. The formal interview was over. We went to the bathroom together and never looked each other in the eye. I thought I was getting it done lickety-split but the worst was yet to come. He asked me to hurry it up cause his coach didn't like 'the guys' to have sex on game day.

"'Does the coach do what I'm doing?' I asked. It was mean and I still wasn't over that girl from the street. The interview was in a shambles. I could have been kneeling in somebody's pee water, but I wanted to get the story. He was Rookie of the Year. He asked me if I was a true sports fan.

"I asked him what that meant.

"'Go deep in the zone.'

"I wanted one thing in return. 'This goes in the interview. No way I'm doing this and not getting something out of it.' He bolted. I looked at myself in the mirror and at that moment I saw my mother's face. She was judgemental. It's not right when you embarrass your dead mother. I was caught in a class war with women, when I should be focused on kicking the patriarchy in the nuts. Never look in a mirror after you've done something truly stupid. You're not going to like who you see. I also learned, never use your power as a woman to enact revenge over another woman. Especially if she is not there to see it. I will not give men anything if it means taking something from another woman."

The ginger in the toque raised her fist in the air, stamped her Martens on the floor and shouted. "Support all women!"

It was obvious to me that she was trying to cover my embarrassment. I shouldn't have told that story. It was a lie, never happened. I wanted to make a good impression. Actually, it's true. You know that, I know they did.

My dad made me a video he wanted me to watch after his funeral. The basement suite on 33rd Street in the 'Toon seemed like the place to view this. It felt like a low-rent funeral home. One of those viewing chapels. They're designed as a fuelling station for grief. Tomorrow night is opening night. It's been "strictly business" in the 'Toon. The director is at his place typing my dialogue. My process doesn't include data entry. The night before last, we didn't have the order of the scenes yet. I gave it my all. The director didn't have any notes. He looked exhausted. I let him lay his head on my lap. We were in the Green Room on a donated couch. Everybody passed out or gone home. He brought his Protestant mouth to my breast and sucked, through my T-shirt. He was my little baby. I knew all of him. I gave him a good feeding. It was the first we'd touched since the alley in Toronto.

The next day everyone was hung-over and we couldn't decide what needed the most work. Everything was kind of up in the air. I never left the stage and I was in the round all the time. I was being full surround judged.

I found myself talking in the washroom with my dad. He wasn't there. I seriously doubt there's an afterlife. Maybe both my parents are avoiding me. The video's on my desktop. Why am I doing this to myself? I put the ear buds in, sit down to watch. I click and there's Dad under his waterfall. There's a lot of amateur camera work. He's talking to me, but like he doesn't know the camera is on. There's shots of the rug. The wall. The light bulb above the door. The video flickers and goes blank.

I hear, "Basketball is taking over because they don't wear helmets. You can see the personalities of the players. You put a helmet on a guy he becomes a robot. Don't get me wrong. I want maximum protection. Especially for my daughter. I'm sorry I said that condoms were like taking a bath with your socks on." This is where he takes a long pause. I used to rush in and save him from his feelings, I can't do nothing for him now. "I didn't deal with your mother's…I could have played better defence on that play." Then he lightens up. He finds a new way to avoid talking about the permanently ruined dinner of our lives. "Let me crystal ball here for a second, will ya? About 90 per cent of the world needs to fuck off, or we'll never get anywhere."

I'm going to commercial. I'm not even two per cent sure the world will fuck off. This last bit is career advice and his way of saying he loves me.

"If life is only five per cent sports, and the rest of it is finding somebody you like to watch television with, you're definitely the person I liked watching television with the most."

Okay, tipping point. I decide to go over to the director's house and tell him I quit. But it's so fucking cold outside. I'll have to do the show.

I don't want to bore you. The show is pretty standard fare. But the thing is there's a naked guy in a jockstrap and a helmet. His job is to walk around the space while I do all the acting. The director said he wanted the Jockstrap Dude 'cause it gave the show a light brushstroke of Greek.

My mom was a writer. I talk about my mom, who she might have been. I don't remember her anymore. First the smell goes and then you're doomed to forget everything. My story is of a girl keeping her spirits up. When you lose your mom that's the best you can do. The director said, "Keep talking. Something's bound to occur to me."

I feel like I'm actually in a pink Cadillac going to hell. I know that I'm kinda here to rep for sports. I sold the director a bag of nothing. Sports aren't that interesting. They're a distraction from the stuff that is interesting. But I promised myself I won't go dark in the 'Toon. I go hard on my life/young woman product. If I can make myself interesting then nobody will care if I ever talk about sports again. The director wanted me to explore the role my mother played in my life choices. I quoted from her note before she left us. I'd memorized it, I speak it privately to myself on the anniversary of her gone-ness:

"Suicide notes are notoriously difficult to write. You want to strike the right tone. No finger pointing. Elevate, go for something tinged with philosophy. There's nothing wrong with a little humour. But jokes do not age well. It will have to be a note of regret, but you're not apologizing for missing a dinner appointment. Think what your friends will miss about you when you're gone. You always brought wine. There must be something more. Ask yourself and for God's sakes be honest. Why? Is it the pain? Is it the emptiness inside? Or is it simply things haven't worked out the way you would have liked? Is it vanity? You have to be sure. This is not a party you're leaving without goodbyes. You're not taking an Irish. Your daughter will never forgive you."

You got that right, My Lady of My Sorrow. Theatre is making me lose my sex drive.

The director is typing this out. I'll give you a highlight reel. I'll just do the goals and the big hits. The skating is what makes hockey beautiful. You only notice the skating live. The skating is a result of spending childhoods on the ice. You have to skate a long time to get good, through all kinds of weather. Here's where I sit down on a Value Village couch and go all method dad.

"In Bible school the only time you were allowed to hold a girl's hand was while skating. I don't know why it was permitted.

You held a girl's hand to prevent your partner from falling. The girls had different skates than the boys and so the gender roles were clear. Boys wore brown hockey skates, girls dressed in white figure skates. Girls' skates had picks on the front end. It was a mystery what you did with them. The action required was different and added to the mystique of everything that was going on. You had to adjust your skating style for the opposite sex. It's a form of dancing. We weren't allowed to dance and so the closest you could get to a girl was during the hour-long skating sessions 7:30 to 9:00 on a Friday night. I was a stylish skater, smooth. I knew how to spray a girl with a moving stop. It was under-appreciated, like pushing a girl into the pool, but still it was a masculine thing and so it had to be done. The girls wore mittens and if a girl liked you enough she would offer her bare hand. If you fell with the bare hands you hurt yourself more. It was a risk that made the skin-on-skin contact all the more precious. You'd lose feeling in your hands due to the cold, but never enough that you lost touch with what you were feeling. Talking was awkward and so a boy did his best to skate faster by pushing the speed limit. It meant the girl would give shrieks of fright or appreciation. She coasted and you did the work. Sometimes you'd get behind the girl and with both hands on her hips you could make her cheeks turn pink in the fast air and the hips were even more exciting than the hands. That would soon be shut down by the supervisor. The excuse was it was bad for safety reasons. But everyone knew why it was forbidden."

I shouted from the kitchen, "The girls were just pretending to be scared."

My dad knew Leviticus. *It is forbidden*. Leviticus is the book in the Bible where all the abominations live, the list of punishments. The permission slips to beat the slave or your wife, but not kill them. Leviticus is the chapter they let the insane write.

Close to the bench you see how young the players are. They have personalities. They spend their lives skating. Every player requires a different kind of coaching. You don't coach the game. You coach the player. Meet your new dad. Hockey players get pulled around by their desires and our desires. They can never outrun their appetites. The crowd has a huge appetite. Our appetites are faster than we can ever be. They're the wagon that pulls us down the street at different velocities. If we get dragged slowly we don't get too cut up. But if they drag fast then you're going to need help.

Every slap shot Bobby Hull took left a bruise the size of your hand. So jockstrap is a farm boy from this area. He's supposed to be the ghost of Bobby Hull. He's never been on a stage before. The jockstrap is my Vanna White with a wicked slap shot. On stage there are some hay bales and farm shit hanging from ropes. He picks stuff up and moves it around. He has a little board that he shoots the puck at. The director said the sound of the boards is the drum that keeps everyone honest. There's another volunteer backstage who has mock sideboards. He slams that with a stick every once in a while. It's pretty cool. I'm commanding an army out there.

Hark, I hear a cell phone ding. The director just texted me and he's coming over. He's not sure about the ending. We need an ending. Endings are tough.

Let me get my hair looking right. I don't like to fuss too much. But everything has to be wrong before it's just right.

The director enters the basement suite. I sit back, how far does the rabbit come into the room? I know what he wants and I'm willing to give it to him. But he won't ask for it. I never ever show a man the menu. He's got a stack of papers in his hand. I'm going to be up all night reading. I place his foot on my lap.

I ask him, "Do you remember where you had your mouth last night?"

"On your breast." He says it like he just passed a feminist exam.

"You don't say tit?"

He shakes his head with shame, I like to reward my director's shame. I start pressing the knots in his feet. All the nerve ends are somewhere around here. I'm going to locate the ending. It's bonus nice to be focusing on another part of the anatomy rather than the dick. I'm growing as a human being.

His body shivers, his leg twitches. The director has a faraway look and says, "There should be a school for endings."

—✳—

The opening night was packed. The director handed me two stubby tickets for free drinks. The jockstrap was surrounded by women. Virginia pops by with a white wine and some kind of weird tofu fake chicken wing. Just when I got a bit of a buzz going here comes the kill. She carries the fake wing in a dainty napkin and offers it to me. Really? I have to eat that? All because of the fucking CPR freight rates? I take one gulp. Okay, give me your best shot. Tell me how terrible I am. Virginia breathes like she's going to dive deeper than usual. There won't be any need for an oxygen tank for her, but I'm feeling deprived. She's dazzling in a blue dress, her hair is electric, her make-up astonishes me. My first thought is how could the director walk away from this? She blurts, "That was amazing. I didn't know what to expect. I was looking for publicity on the show and never saw any, but this hit me right between the gut and my heart. Totally winning. As a woman I wanted to stand up and cheer. Good for you. That took a lot of courage. And

Talent. I know you have people who want to tell you how good you were, but I wanted to share one little story with you. He wasn't rookie of the year. He was a gold medalist from Surrey. A downhill guy. People who live dangerously have strange tastes. There's some kind of cheerleader thing left over from high school that makes me rah rah rah, Peter is our man, if he can't do it no one can. I blamed myself and tonight I stopped that. Thank you."

When the kick to the nuts you're expecting doesn't come, it's so refreshing. I tell her she looks stunning and thank her. I want to kiss her and hold her and say how sorry I am she was dropped 'cause some guy didn't like her work. I also wanted to look at her. Women are magic. Maybe this was a revenge look? Theatre was a funny battleground. I could see that. I told her that the director would really appreciate hearing from her. "I know he really respects your work and your opinion." When in Rome, baby. She nods and breathes again and downs the rest of her glass. I step back to give the director some room. I watch them do the air kiss. I can see her pain and hurt and she pushes through and gives the asshole his due. So this is the theatre, huh? It feels like high school with free drink tickets. It's artificial Christmas. I like Virginia. I want to take her back to the funeral parlour. I want to hear how bad it was with King Peter. But my director has to be protected. Tonight, he's mine. I step forward so that Virginia can do her strategic retreat. She smiles with gratitude. I salute her. Away she heads out into the dark forest with just her basket and her cape. I wish her kind wolves and rich grandmothers.

My director bought a new shirt for the show. You know how they get folded into their tight little packages. His still had the fold lines visible on the back. He had product in the hair. He really put out for this one. He gave me a card with a picture of Marilyn Monroe leaning against a pink Cadillac. On the back, "Thanks for not OD-ing on sleeping pills. You're a STAR! I wish life was just one long rehearsal with you."

I felt like a dependent little suck. I clapped my two hands over my ears, "How good was I? I don't want to know."

He grips my wrists like precious china, pulls my hands slowly away from my ears. Slo-mo. He fights me for the lime-light. We wrestle back and forth. He puts me in a headlock. Not a good look for today. I break free. I fake knee him in the balls. I know it hurt him a little. My bad. "Safety before passion," my acting teacher used to say.

My director says, "Once I acted in a play with Tony Nappo. He's the guy who posts all this random shit, his personal brand is honesty. If a woman is in danger he'll punch the bad guy in the face. I wouldn't want him to punch me in the face. He's funny, a warm guy, he just hates Nazis. Do I come across as a Nazi? After a particularly great show for him, he was very honest in his performance. He said, 'A show is only as good as its worst actor.' He never said that was me. But I never went on stage again. I lost my dream of being an actor, but I found my girl in the pink Caddy. You're my rookie of the year."

I just told my life story to a bunch of strangers and they gave me a Saskatoon standing ovation. Everyone gets to their feet to clap and combines that with grabbing their coats and heading for the exits. They're worried their cars won't start. It's so fucking cold I feel their pain. After I left the stage I stuck my head out the door. It was a symphony of windshield scraping.

I don't have to fuck the director to keep this job. My performance did that for me. I'm starting to feel myself again, only way less needy. I say goodbye to stage manager woman. She wears a pink toque with DON'T EVEN on it. She buries me in a hug that lasts a long time, "You were so good. I want to adopt you. You added three more 'fucks' to the show than normal. Try not to use PUSSY in a pejorative manner. That's all your notes. See you tomorrow, Beauty."

I figured this out. Theatre is a kind of orphanage. Everybody says I got my fanny from my mother. I thank my ancestors and head for the exit. My mother is definitely hanging around somewhere. I have to keep a sharp eye out for her. What's the one thing the cold can't kill? Cold hard lust. That's some Leviticus shit right there.

Rod Carley

THE LAND OF
THE LIZARD-PEOPLE

Enjoying a family reunion is the ultimate improbability.

Specifically, the annual summer gathering starring all of Neil's hapless relatives. He needs to appreciate the effort I put in to not being a serial killer. I want to strangle the lot of them. I drink coffee first thing in the morning to help *them* live longer. The Price family is into strange cults, all of them – with the exception of Neil. I can almost handle the tenets of sacred geometry, and the notion that our eyeballs are shaped like mystical fish bladders, but the weirdness that Neil's family believes in drives me bananas. They're mad enough to make a druid start a forest fire. Can one family all be deprived of oxygen at birth? I worry that Neil is genetically predisposed to their galloping insanity and I'll wake up one morning to find him sacrificing Salinger, our Jack Russell Terrier, to his garden gnomes. I'd like to lock them in a room for eternity – relatives and gnomes.

Neil's younger sister Violet is a botanist, having spent the last 30 years studying tree architecture – poetic botany, she calls it. She chooses tropical plants much like herself: strange, odd looking, and stinky. Trees that walk, vines that dance, orchids that kill, a palm with a leaf the size of a catering tent, floating seaweed with an inflatable bladder, a flower that smells like rotting flesh, and other weird French-kissing plants. Neil says she sees poetry in the unusual habits of rare plants in the same way a person who loves literature is fascinated by the cadence of poetry versus the narrative of a novel. To my way of thinking, she's the original crazy cat lady. She is also a member of a horticultural cult known as the Church of All Plants, based on a 1962 counterculture science fiction novel, *Stranger from a Green Land,* about a human raised by trees in a tropical rain forest, who comes back to society and challenges the status quo view of sex, religion, and lawn care. Violet dresses like an ageing flower child, waves a willow wand, and talks to trees. She married a birch tree named Herb after successfully petitioning to have the tree granted the same legal rights as a human. When I told her I didn't have a green thumb, she said it was because my roots didn't go deep enough. "You're barking up the wrong tree," I said.

Neil's Uncle Ned is a Pythagorean, meaning exactly what the name implies. He worships the geometry of Pythagoras. The ancient Greek mathematician, besides loving triangles, also believed in reincarnation. When Uncle Ned was a teenager he witnessed a man beating a dog, and called for the beating to stop, not because beating a dog in itself was a cruel act, but because he recognized in the yelps of the dog the voice of that of his deceased grandfather. Uncle Ned is also addicted to hallucinogenic mushrooms. He believes that Salinger is the reincarnation of the famous dead author. At last year's family fiasco, I told him Salinger is currently writing a sequel called *The Fetcher in the Rye.*

"Be serious, Rudolph," he exclaimed and stormed off in three different directions.

Neil's parents are obsessed with the Heaven's Gate cult – not the embarrassingly awful movie responsible for destroying the Western, killing independent film making, and forcing Kris

Kristofferson to never leave his day job again, but a bizarre religious cult based on the Book of Revelation. Neil's parents believe the Earth is doomed to be "recycled" and the only way to survive is to escape from the Earth itself. For the past 25 years, Neil's father has been building a spaceship in his barn using old tires, refrigerators, tin foil, and recycled cans. He steals the recyclables out of his neighbours' blue boxes.

"How many tuna cans will it take to get to Mars?" I asked him last summer.

"Ask Ned," he replied, missing the joke. "He's the math expert. Last I saw him he was measuring some twigs branching out of Herb."

But it is Neil's big brother – and I mean big – who is the cherry on the top of the nutbar sundae. Wing-nut is obsessed with lizard-people (his real name is Walter Price but I call him Wing-nut in front of his back). The idea of shapeshifting lizards taking human forms in a plot to rule the world dates back to the early '80s, coming from the disturbed mind of David Ick, a certifiable nutbar who first rose to fame playing British football. After receiving one too many balls to the head he quit professional sports, becoming a spokesperson for the Green Party of England and Wales. His mad speeches made communists look tame by comparison. On a cold day in January while Operation Desert Storm bombed the crap out of Kuwait, Icky, as I prefer to call him, was busy hugging a cluster of trees in Kew Gardens. A bolt of lightning must have struck him in the head because, from that moment on, he's dedicated his life to warning mankind that the earth is secretly controlled by alien lizard-people.

In Canada, Wing-nut carries the alien-lizard conspiracy torch. Neil has one of Wing-nut's old Green Party election signs hanging in the garage as a souvenir. It reads THE PRICE IS

RIGHT. Beneath the text is the image of an iguana in a business suit within a red circle with a diagonal slash through it.

"Lizard-people are cold-blooded, humanoid reptilians who have the power to shapeshift into human form," Wing-nut explains to me for the umpteenth time at this year's reunion.

Encroaching on other conspiracy theorists' territory, Wing-nut claims that lizards are behind secret societies like the Freemasons, the Illuminati, and the cast of *Friends*. He's convinced that lizard-people filled Canadian television programming in the 1970s: Al Waxman on the *King of Kensington*, Bruno Gerussi and Robert Clothier on *The Beachcombers*, *The Friendly Giant*, *Mr. Dressup*, and anyone ever connected to *Front Page Challenge*.

"They made us dumb by getting us hooked on Canadian TV," he says.

I do not know anyone who ever got hooked on Canadian television programming.

Wing-nut says there are more lizard-people living amongst us than we are aware. "Keep in mind that this isn't counting all the people who, in their heart of hearts, believe that lizard-people exist but are nervous they will be found out if they publicly disclose their beliefs," he whispers to me while inhaling a slice of Neil's home-made rhubarb pie. "It's more dangerous than the communist witch-hunt." If alien-lizards pose such a threat to global security, funny how a modern-day Joe McCarthy hasn't risen from the ashes to launch a full alien-lizard senate investigation. I asked Wing-nut that. He replied, "It's obvious. McCarthy was secretly a lizard-person." He can't hear me scream inside my head.

"How do I know if someone is a lizard-person?" I ask. Humouring Wing-nut is the only way to avoid the rest of Neil's family. I tried playing sick last year and was inundated by foul-tasting birch tea remedies, missives stating I was a peasant during the Black Plague in a previous life, and repeated warnings to recycle and pack my things.

"There are numerous ways to spot lizard-people in a crowd," Wing-nut hisses, moistly flicking his tongue.

"How?" I say, already knowing the answer.

"Green, hazel, or blue eyes that can change colour like a chameleon," he says. "Keen eyesight and hearing, red hair or reddish hair, unexplained scars on the body, low blood pressure, psychic abilities, a sense of not belonging to the human race, and a capability to disrupt electrical appliances – they're all signs."

The toaster rarely works when Neil is in the kitchen. But that's because he forgets to plug it in.

"The Prime Minister is a lizard-person," Wing-nut grunts.

"Doesn't he have dark brown hair?" I say. "How can *he* be a lizard-person?"

"He dyes his hair."

"Trudeau's secretly a redhead?"

"You betcha. According to his doctors, he brags about his low blood pressure. He doesn't wear glasses or a hearing aid. Three days after he took office, there was a spike in UFO sightings in his home province of Quebec. That guy on the CBC who has that science show claims that Trudeau told him he'd seen a UFO and communicated with it telepathically. His aides say he has an uncanny ability to assassinate flies with an elastic band from the doorway of the Prime Minister's office. His father knew a guy who ran Area 51. Castro was involved *and* Barbra Streisand. That's about as reptilian as you can get."

"Ah, well, that just about says it all, doesn't it?" I'm ready to head back to the motel.

Wing-nut leans in, holding his fork up like a trident. "What makes lizard-people lizard people is something that you can't see," he whispers. I wish a summer breeze was leaning in. Wing-nut reeks.

I nod in understanding, pretending to connect with my inner Buddha. "Ah, so it's about the soul inhabiting the body, not the physical body alone," I say languidly. I got in touch with my inner self last month. Then I unfriended him on Facebook and shamed him on social media. I hold my hands out to the side, palms up. "The inner self of the lizard-person."

"Yes!" he shouts, spitting rhubarb in my face. "Now you've got it!"

"So, what do lizard-people want?" I ask, scanning the backyard for Neil. Family members are dispersing. Uncle Ned is still drawing triangles on the driveway.

"World domination and cheaper Tim Hortons' coffee." Wing-nut's mouth, throat, and chest begin to vibrate. I think of William Shatner battling a Gorn on *Star Trek*.

Aside from *his* paranoiac brain, I ask Wing-nut where lizard-people come from. I can see Neil collecting his Tupperware through the kitchen window.

"The Ninth Dimension. The constellation of Draco," says Wing-nut, attempting to wrap his arms around himself. He gets about as far as his elbows.

Draco is the constellation that is allegedly shaped like a dragon or, if you go with its Latin name *Draconem*, means "huge serpent." It's the eighth largest constellation. On a clear summer night we can see Draco at the cottage.

"Reptoids from Draco are very tall and have retractable wings." Wing-nut demonstrates. He resembles an obese rhubarb-dripping pterodactyl. He fixes his gaze on me. "Though there are some theories that reptoids come from other systems like Sirius and Orion too."

"And they send messages on Sirius radio?"

"Yes! You're finally getting it." He is overjoyed at my progress. "Sirius radio is their broadcast system for secret messaging and brainwashing. Basically, they're all aliens too."

Lizard-people have been visiting Earth since the day the Serpent first showed up in Genesis. "A reptoid in disguise," Wing-nut assures me. They have been breeding with humans, which has resulted in more lizard-people, and more humans with the potential to be lizard-people.

Most lizard-people are usually A-listers. The list of alleged lizard-people celebrities includes Celine Dion, Wayne Gretzky, Anne of Green Gables, Ben Mulroney, and the Chrises Pratt, Pine, Hadfield, and Hemsworth. Justin Bieber, too, among others. I did watch a Justin Bieber video accidentally at the gym in which his eyes seemed to shift and turn like a reptile. Chris Hadfield is the most promising candidate – an astronaut singing David Bowie's "Space Oddity" in outer space has certain lizard-alien potential. Plus, he was born in Sarnia, a chemical city choking on refineries and smog, the perfect incubation site for science fiction lizard disasters. Ironically, Hitler was not a lizard-person. He just thought the Jews were.

"Could I secretly be a lizard-person?" I ask, all mock wonderment.

"Possibly, Rudolph." Wing-nut's eyebrows draw together. "Do you like the taste of flies?"

I stroke my goatee, deep in thought. "Deer, black, or shad?" I ask as if awaiting the answer to a cancer diagnosis.

"Only you know the truth," he replies gravely, backing away, and leaving in a hurry.

I guess there are worse things I could be than a humanoid lizard with plans for world domination. Neil's nephew is definitely not a lizard-person. Last week, he called the police because his fake ID didn't arrive.

A week later, I read an article in *The New Yorker* about ancient lizard limb muscles found in a human fetus. Babies in the womb have extra lizard-like muscles in their hands that they lose before they are born. Probably the oldest, albeit fleeting, remnants of evolution seen in humans yet, some Harvard biologists say. The biologists date them as 250 million years old – a relic from when reptiles transitioned to mammals and Betty White first got into acting.

"Humans have lost the lizard muscles because we don't need them," explained the Harvard biologist leading the study. "So, there is no danger of us becoming super-human."

This isn't Wing-nut talking; these are serious, lab coat-wearing scientists paid to hunch over a microscope. So, while there hasn't been a humanoid lizard born yet or transformed by a serum like the Lizard in *The Amazing Spider-Man*, the human uterus is showing signs of some really creepy reptile ancestors. Might Wing-nut actually be on to something? Could I have the remnants of a dinosaur's thumb? It all sounds like the hitch-hiker's guide to evolution.

I go deeper down the rabbit-lizard hole.

Researchers from a Sleep Team in the Nevada desert recently confirmed that lizards exhibit two sleep states similar to humans. Bearded dragons, in a hidden research lab near Area 51, experienced both slow-wave sleep and REM sleep patterns.

I begin counting lizards in my sleep. I have a paranoid thought: what if a lizard-alien on a faraway planet is counting me? My life is turning into a Philip K. Dick short story.

Up until this point, when I think of reptiles, the image that comes to mind is a garter snake slithering through the grass at the cottage or the little lizards that climb the walls at my sister's rental *casa* in Mexico.

"Can lizards really feel or display emotions?" I asked Salinger's vet during my last visit.

"Lizards do demonstrate basic emotions, fear and aggression for instance," she replied while injecting Salinger with his rabies shot. "But they also indicate pleasure when offered food."

"So does my cat, but she's just ensuring her needs are met. When I fall asleep on the couch, I wake up and she's wearing a bib and pouring ketchup on my wrist."

Salinger's vet gave me her, *Are you telling that same stupid joke?* look again.

"C'mon, lizards expressing love?" I said with polite opposition.

"I don't know if it is love," she explained, all science, "but lizards appear to like some people more than others. They also show the most emotions of reptiles, appearing to show pleasure when being stroked."

Lizards do get a bad rap in movies, comics, and TV. From Godzilla to the alien reptiles of *V* to that tyrannosaurus chasing Jeff Goldblum in *Jurassic Park*, they're portrayed as scary, sneaky, and unknowable – much like the administration at the college.

I go even deeper down the lizard hole – I've become a paranoid miner looking for evidence of the fake moon landing in Sudbury.

Most lizards have movable eyelids, unlike snakes, although some cannot blink, and have to lick their eyeballs instead, which is preferable to watching Salinger lick his penis. Some lizards even have eyes that shoot blood to frighten predators. I bet Chris Hadfield can shoot blood out of *his* eyes. He survived a spacewalk after his left eye suddenly slammed shut. Supposedly, a big ball of oily anti-fog solution, meant to keep his astronaut visor clear, built up over his eye because, without gravity, his tears had nowhere to go. The ball got so big it spread like a waterfall over the bridge of his nose into his other eye. He was completely blind outside his spaceship. Nevertheless, he warded off primal terror, lived to sing the tale, and finished the mission. Also, Chris Hadfield seems like a really nice guy, so it only makes sense that he's a giant lizard underneath.

Lizards smell with their tongues, shed their skin in large flakes, and can regrow their tails if attacked. Lizards can walk on water and can reproduce by themselves. I never understood how or why chameleons changed colour until recently. I thought it was just about camouflage – it's not. Switching hues reflects emotion, according to a back issue of *National Geographic* I read in my doctor's waiting room while waiting to have a skin tag removed. Skin tags are not a characteristic of lizard-people. Changing colours sends different messages to other chameleons – a form of lizard texting and sexting; a "baby, you make me hot-blooded" sort of thing.

―⁙―

Ranging from the crashing waves of the Pacific Ocean to the tranquil turquoise seas of the Caribbean, Mexico has more than enough beaches to keep Canadian expats, who aren't afraid of drug cartels, happy.

"What you see in the news is mainland Mexico," Jimmy explained to me a few years back. "We are far away from the rest of the country."

JoJo and Jimmy rent a small rundown two-bedroom beachfront *casa* in Cerritos, south of Baja Sur, miles away from Cancun. It's a rugged spit of land flanked by the Pacific and the equally wild Sea of Cortez. The little surfer town isn't entirely off the radar, but it has a ramshackle, low-key vibe that suits Jimmy's bohemian hippie fantasy life. Development has remained relatively tame and the beach is blissfully free of high rises. There are only a couple of large hotels so it isn't overrun by tourists, and most of the town consists of a mix of local fishermen (the *pescadores locales*) and surfers. Fresh fish and seafood are available in thatch-shaped spots called *enramadas*, which line the beach. Still, there are enough tattoo shops, yoga classes, and fresh juice vendors to keep JoJo happy. The ocean is safe for swimming, but the big breaks mean that most people come armed with a board, with the exception of Neil and me, who come armed with books and sunscreen. The town is also home to a massive population of sea turtles which nest on its shores in season. They wait until the full moon to come ashore to lay their eggs. The higher tide takes them further onto the shore, where it's better for them to make their nests. The reef offshore is protected so the sea life makes for amazing snorkelling possibilities for Neil. Best of all, it is a natural barrier to sharks. For me, other than the sun and the sea, it's all about cold beer and margaritas, cheap eats, and sunsets on the beach.

The nearest airport to Cerritos is La Paz International Airport. It is only a five-hour direct flight from Toronto, and customs is a breeze.

I am going to run with the new identity given to me by Juan, the La Paz customs and immigration officer who, after checking my passport signature, dubbed me "Mr. X."

The terrible jokes about my handwriting by immigration officials around the globe has gotten stale. I have heard all their questions:

"Has it always been this bad?"

"How did you manage in school?"

"Pouvez-vous réellement lire cela? Eres disléxico?"

The real winner doesn't come from the mouth of an immigration officer but from a loud Texan behind us in line: "My writing looked like that when I was two," he bellows, pointing at my passport so that everyone in the airport can see.

"At least I can write," I fire back. No, I don't. I want to, though.

"Handwriting *el malo es un sign of inteligencia superior*," I manage to say in broken Spanish to a second mustachioed officer.

"*Al menos puedes leerlo*," he says and waves us through to find our luggage.

"C'mon, Professor X," Neil smirks. "Shave your head and you're set."

Professor X does have possibilities. I could be the creator of the X-Men. All I need is a wheelchair, a conservative blue suit, and the voice of Patrick Stewart. I am, however, lacking in the telepathic powers and scientific genius departments.

Professor Xavier dreams of peaceful coexistence between mutants and humanity; for me it will have to be humans and lizard-people. Maybe I can open a school for higher learning to help me reach out to young lizard-people and help mold them into responsible lizard-people who only use their powers for the benefit of all mankind.

"You're addicted to that thing," I say to Neil as we wait by the baggage carousel. He's preoccupied with checking his phone.

"What are you talking about?" he replies. "I'm messaging Jimmy to say we've landed safely."

Neil is in love with his phone, although he won't admit it. The longer I spend on my phone, the more I think I could be doing something more useful, as if I would otherwise be reading a Russian novel.

⚊⁄₁ᐟ⚊

JoJo and Jimmy pick us up out front in a bright orange Jeep rental. It is a two-hour drive to Cerritos due to road construction on the worst four-lane highway in Mexico. Jimmy has the top down. The dry wind blows into the back seat causing my ears to ring. I suffer from crooked inner ear canals which leads to a wicked wax build-up. I have them syringed before I fly. I make a candle for my niece from the wax each Christmas. Syringing, chewing gum, and wearing ear plugs for takeoff and landing prevent my eardrums from exploding.

The rough desert terrain stretches out in all directions interrupted by patches of dramatic jungle scenery and white sand beaches. Jimmy pulls over and the three of them take a quick dip in a *cenote*, a freshwater swimming hole created by a sinkhole in the limestone bedrock. For the first time I notice he's sporting a new sea turtle tattoo on his right bicep.

"What about crocodiles?" I ask, nervously scanning the surface while they laugh, dive, bob, float, splash, and otherwise enjoy each other.

"This is a busy tourist route," Jimmy yells back. "Mexican crocodiles stay away from it."

"They're listed as a 'Least Concern' species," JoJo shouts.

I am not convinced. That was the view Democrats had of Trump in 2015.

Back in the Jeep, we pass by a Mayan ruin. I feel a deep reverence for the local culture and history, although their calendar begs a rethink. The Mayan calendar resembles an Oreo cookie. The Oreo calendar tells us not to worry and just dip ourselves in milk.

"As close to paradise as you'll find," says Jimmy breezily, looking over his shoulder at me. "The best kept secret in *Me-hi-co*." He turns onto the winding dirt road that leads down to their tiny rental *casa*. "Wind chill of 33 degrees Celsius today," he announces with a mirthful laugh.

As much as Jimmy likes to imagine he's roughing it, JoJo makes sure they indulge themselves. They have a housekeeper, which they don't have in Canada. The *casa* is spotless. We throw our stuff down on the floor in the guest room and I quickly change into my trunks for an ocean dip.

"Best keep your things off the floor," advises Jimmy, passing by the open doorway. "Scorpions sometimes crawl into things. They're not big enough to kill you but they still pack a sting. Make sure you check your flip-flops in the morning."

Wearing flip-flops in bed is a done deal.

The sun in Mexico is brutal, and I am a perfect storm for developing skin cancer – a triptych of fair skin, a constellation of moles on my back, and the wheezing ozone layer. I lather on waterproof sunscreen and SPF protection first thing in the morning. I spend most of the day slippery to the touch, applying and reapplying the messy sunscreen. I learned the hard way last year not to be fooled by overhead clouds and cool breezes. My skin got so tight I thought *I* was in danger of becoming a lizard-person. Neil is naturally dark-skinned so he is more protected. The bastard.

Jimmy has cleared a path for those who visit, becoming the Expat King of Cerritos. He took Spanish lessons at the local school last year but quit shortly thereafter when it interfered with his beer-drinking schedule. He speaks Spanish in the present tense only.

"I'm living in the moment. Mindfulness, *amigos*. Not living in the past or future," he rationalizes as he cracks open a beer at nine in the morning.

Yesterday's hang-over is today's first beer.

"It's less expensive to live down here," he grins. Jimmy has been trying to convince Neil and me to retire to Cerritos for the past three years.

"Fruits and vegetables are cheap, cheap, cheap," adds JoJo.

"You sound like a parakeet," I say, wiping sunscreen off my glasses.

The pair of them love to cook and entertain. JoJo reads and writes her books, takes yoga classes, and continues with her Spanish lessons. Salsa and Tortilla, the cocker spaniels, are shaved to cool them down. Their paws resemble Edwardian spats.

"I love to grill," Jimmy announces at least three times a day. He sounds like Tony the Tiger. "For everyone."

Note to self, meeting my brother-in-law's expat friends will soon be on the agenda.

The first grilling happens that night.

Expats love fiestas. The guest list includes a core of now-permanent residents and four snowbirds for whom the Cerritos beach is their part-time winter haven. Cerritos is a welcoming community, where you make friends easily whether you want to or not.

One of the expats, Al, is a former New York firefighter who took an early retirement package after 9/11. Al is used to the heat. His claim to fame is that an actor in the movie *Reservoir Dogs* served with him in Manhattan's Little Italy during the early '80s.

"That's right. Mr. Pink used to pull people out of burning buildings for a living," Al broadcasts loudly over drinks. Al says everything loudly – he is a walking fire alarm.

After 9/11, the oddball character actor returned to his fire-fighting platoon and worked 12-hour shifts alongside Al, digging and sifting through the rubble from the World Trade Center looking for survivors.

"It's hard to visualize," I say, "Steve Buscemi on a firefighter calendar. He looks like a cross between Don Knotts and a bottle opener."

Can Steve Buscemi be a lizard-person? He is such an obvious choice I rule him out immediately.

"Just so I'm clear," says Al, flexing a bicep. "Steve may look like a bug-eyed cigarette, but he's a total bad ass." Al can say that because he has the rugged good looks of Steve McQueen in *The Towering Inferno*. He is one of those annoying guys who can change a tire blindfolded, without a jack.

Al's wife, Brenda, is a former fire department badge bunny. She listened to scanners, chased sirens, made loaves and loaves of banana bread and brought them to firehouses, and watched Al from the sidelines, showing up at the blazes he was fighting dressed in her best man-bait attire.

"The early '80s were the War Years," Al says, dropping his voice an octave. He speaks of the 80s as if the Vietnam War had come to the streets of New York City. He reminds me of that older F.B.I. agent in *Die Hard*, the one with the bad skin.

"Because of the recession," Al elaborates, "people were burning down empty buildings for insurance money. Landlords abandoned buildings because they couldn't afford to keep tenants there. It was nuts. We'd get a call, go to a building, come back and get another call."

Brenda eventually tracked Al down, showing up at his local "bar for badges" and made her move. Things moved from hot to inferno very quickly.

"John Mellencamp should've written that song about us, not Jack and Diane," she says without moving her mouth.

"Our fire was hotter than any backdraft," Al winks. He imitates a siren. I swear a pelican stopped fishing to listen. Fanning the flames further, I learned they had their first tryst in Al's station pumper.

"Just like William Baldwin and Jennifer Jason Leigh," giggles Brenda with the laughter of a 15-year-old. All very unsettling coming from a 55-year-old sunbaked trophy wife. Now an ageing beach bunny hooked on Botox, Brenda opts for olive oil instead of sunscreen.

The other expat couple introduce themselves as Christopher and Elizabeth Van Prattle, a pair of retired Dutch international IT consultants turned Mexican real estate developers. They are fit, casually but fashionably well-dressed, and exude a kind of ease that only rich people can. In another life they could have been Wimbledon tennis doubles champions. They are JoJo and Jimmy's landlords.

"We pay only two hundred dollars in tax on our condo," Elizabeth shares, nursing her second margarita. "Instead of paying eight thousand in property taxes, we travel."

"You guys should look into it, Neil," Christopher joins in. "Real estate deals are everywhere. And the farther from the beach you go, the better deals you can find. It's still a reasonable walk or quick bike ride. Head farther west, into the local Mexican neighbourhoods, and you pay even less. I've got a two-bedroom bungalow next to the beach listed at $199,000." He glances over his shoulder. "A few blocks inland from the water, but still a pleasant walk, is a two-bedroom unit for $109,000.

Now if you want real luxury, I can find that for you too. We're building a condo compound on the beach with resort amenities. Daily house cleaning service, the works. Available for $399,000 – and it comes furnished. American dollars of course."

Of course. Christopher and Elizabeth are the kind of people I hate in my real world.

Two of the snowbirds are from Michigan. They both dye their hair black, that fake black that resembles a pair of cheap Halloween fright wigs from Value Village.

"They look like they bleach their faces," I whisper to Neil.

He's short, she's tall. I can't remember their real names. No one can.

"How come men get called hot silver foxes when they age and women just get hot flashes?" says the tall spouse.

"Men naturally age better," says Al, catching his reflection in his glass.

"Men only look distinguished with grey hair if they already looked distinguished before," replies the tall spouse curtly. "Take George Clooney. Not Woody Allen."

Or the short spouse. He could be cast as a hobbit with a black mullet.

"Grey hair is ageing naturally?" he asks rhetorically. "I've had a hip replacement, open heart surgery, and chemo. If I aged naturally, I'd be dead."

Personally, I think a house looks best with some snow on the roof. The other snowbirds are Ricky and Sally who rent a bungalow beside Jimmy and JoJo. They also share the pool and outdoor common area. Ricky is an East Londoner that no one can understand. There is a lot of nodding in agreement whenever Ricky is speaking.

"Yewe Knadians are tewe palite," Ricky spits. "If this plass err packed wit' me mates, they'd be ping pong tiddly an' garden hosin' and peas and carroting inna bushes, thay wood. And Posh and Beckin' wit' the local birds."

It is a job for Alan Turing trying to decipher Ricky's cockney accent. Ricky laughs himself into a spasmodic fit and almost swallows his cigar – one of those big Freudian stogies, the smoking, sexting kind. By day, Ricky lounges and bakes by the pool, blasting classic pub tunes and modern hip-hop on his iPad – imagine Sydney Greenstreet in a Speedo. Ricky is into TikTok. He tapes himself dancing and posts the alarming videos on Facebook. It can put you off tacos for life.

Sally, Ricky's wife, is the spitting image of Michael Palin during his Monty Python drag days. Sally rarely remembers how she got home from the bar the night before.

The sun sets at 6:40, a whimsical tiger-tail swirl of colour. JoJo lights an assortment of candles and tiki torches, setting the mood while keeping the bugs away. Jimmy pours us all a Mexican red wine and serves up his feast, consisting of Mexican barbecued chicken marinated in achiote paste and a healthy salad with romaine lettuce, black beans, cherry tomatoes, avocado, queso fresco, and cilantro in an avocado-yogurt dressing.

After dinner, the rum and tequila come out. I am going to spend the next seven days of my vacation self-quarantined in bed with a Mexican hang-over.

To quarantine or not to quarantine is the topic of post-dinner conversation.

"Did y'ear about tha crewz hip?" says Ricky, lighting up another fat stogie.

We all nod until Al finally says, "What are you talking about, mate?"

"Crewz hip," repeats Ricky.

"Crew zip?" says Al.

"Crewz hip!" repeats Ricky again, waving his cigar for emphasis. "Crewz hip!"

"Cruise ship?" asks JoJo. She is a contestant on *Wheel of Fortune for Dummies.*

"Tha crewz hip off tha roast, aye."

Christopher steps in with the diplomacy of a U.N. translator. "There's a Norwegian cruise ship stranded in the Caribbean Sea off the coast of Cancun."

"Isn't there a flu bug on board or thomething?" thays Brenda, thlurring her words, well on her way to a fifth margarita grand thlam.

"Something like that," says Elizabeth. I detect a slight trace of condescension. "Twenty crew members and passengers are sick. The captain wants to dock in Cancun so they can disembark."

You will never catch me on a six-storey cruise ship. There is something about a mass-market luxury cruise that's unbearably sad. A giant mall and buffet table housed in a giant sardine can floating on water with no land in sight. It is not my idea of a relaxing vacation. Your capacities for choice, error, regret, and despair? All are removed. Plus, I don't want to see seasick passengers dressed in cheap formal dinner wear. Jimmy says you are too high up to hear the ship's big engines. I am sure I would be the exception, developing an unnerving spinal throb, losing my balance and falling overboard.

"Mexican authorities are trying to decide whether to let the captain land or not," explains Christopher. "The WHO is weighing in."

"Who?" Brenda says, sloppily.

"Exactly," says Christopher.

"Who?" repeats Brenda, stamping her bare feet in the sand. Small children and faded beach bunnies have a lot in common.

"Of course, that's their job," says Christopher, with a quick conspiratorial wink to the rest of us.

"Who'th job?" says Brenda. It hasn't dawned on her yet that she's the only one not in on the joke.

"Precisely," says Christopher.

"C'mon, stop it! What is the name of the organization?"

"Not what…WHO," says Jimmy, joining in, his old radio days timing still on point.

"That'th what I'm trying to find out!" Brenda screams, knocking her glass over in the process. Salsa and Tortilla race to the accident site.

"World Health Organization," says Elizabeth drily. "They arrive at a decision tomorrow."

"All because of a Norwegian flu?" asks JoJo. Young adult fiction writers and current events rarely go together.

"It's not the flu. It's something else," says Neil. "A virus of some sort."

"Anyone want a Corona?" says Jimmy, weaving his way to the outdoor bar fridge.

"Sure," shouts Al. "Leave them out there. Give them supplies and let them refuel, but don't let them land. They can go back to Norway and let the Norwegians deal with it. If Cancun gets sick, we'll all get sick."

"You're being paranoid, Al," says Jimmy. "Not everything is a disaster waiting to happen." He takes a long swig of his Corona.

"Once a firefighter always a firefighter," says Al. "The WHO should quarantine the entire ship."

"Is Roger Daltrey on board?" It's Sally perking up, "That's my generation," and she passes out.

"Tomorrow is another day," says Jimmy.

"Leth go thkinny dipping," Brenda pipes up. She stands up, starts to spin, and gets caught up in her halter top. "Fuck!"

Ricky begins stripping off his shorts.

The sound of an ATV pulling up on the beach.

Saved by the sound of a Northern Ontario off-road bush engine. Salsa and Tortilla bark up a tsunami. JoJo doesn't make them wear their anti-barking collars in Mexico.

"Shut up!" Jimmy yells.

The dogs quiet down.

"Hey, Fred!" Jimmy shouts to the driver, sounding more like a star-struck hockey fan than his usual Mexican chill self.

A man clad in Bermuda shorts and a pink golf shirt jumps off the ATV with the ease of a Hollywood action-movie terrorist. He takes off his helmet, revealing a fierce, craggy Nordic blond handsomeness – Rutger Hauer hiding out in Mexico. He's tall and physically fit with a striking yet casually commanding presence.

But it is the man's foreignness, his Europeanese, which is immediately brought into play, a symbol of something sinister and coldly cynical, like an uber-shark waiting just beyond the reef.

"Hola, buenas tardes, mis amigos, com ova tu noche?" the man says, his Spanish perfect. This Foreign Fred is a curious specimen. His mouth smiles. His eyes do not.

"No podría ser major," replies Christopher with another wink accompanied by a grin. I sense a secret code.

"Couldn't be better," Jimmy repeats for my benefit. *"Puedo conseguirte una cerveza?"*

"Gracias." Foreign Fred grabs a seat with his back to the casa.

"'Ow er things droppin' frown at tha nuclear sub?" says Ricky.

"Busy night," replies Foreign Fred.

I almost cough up a filling. He understands Ricky's accent.

"Monster margarita night and a full moon," he says.

I look up at the night sky over the ocean. The moon is keeping us company with its buttermilk glow. I learn that Foreign Fred became a permanent resident in Cerritos 10 years ago, opening a popular expat beach bar.

"'Owl and meow." Ricky leers and gives Brenda a nudge.

"You remember JoJo's brother, Rudy, and his partner, Neil?" says Jimmy. He hands Foreign Fred a Corona with lime.

"Ah, of course, how are things in the land of ice and snow?" Foreign Fred responds with a deliberate touch of self-aware drollery.

"Cold," says Neil, "Glad to be here."

"Better than on that cruise chip," I say. "Guess we'll know more tomorrow."

Foreign Fred gives me a disconcerting look. "Even if they do dock in Cancun, no one's coming here, *Rudrigo*. We're Mexico's best kept secret, right, Jimmy boy?"

"*Apuesto, mi amigo*," Jimmy agrees. "*Es un lugar excelente*." It is an awkward attempt at cracking Foreign Fred and Christopher's secret code.

Best kept secret? Stop the Mayan calendar. An expat bar in a remote beach town would be the perfect cover for a drug-dealing cartel.

I know enough from watching *60 Minutes* that Mexico's drug cartel history is one of violent splits and constant fighting between themselves as they battle for supremacy. Cartel have already turned Cancun and Playa del Carmen into a deadly war zone. Foreign Fred is alarmingly right. The authorities won't give Cerritos a second look. The village *fuerza policial* consist of two uniformed *oficiales* riding around in a golf cart with a goat.

"What if Foreign Fred is secretly a drug lord?" I say to Neil later, after checking under the sheets for scorpions.

"He's not," Neil yawns.

"Hear me out. What if he's the notorious 'El Mencho,' murdering and mutilating his enemies, stuffing them in bin bags, and dumping their remains in abandoned wells in the desert. There's that dried-up old well just a few miles outside of town. We passed it on our way in from the airport. I thought nothing of it then, but what if Foreign Fred is a balaclava-sporting killer?"

The recent spate of killings in the news increased my anxiety about travelling to Mexico. Last week, terrified tourists were sent running for cover when a lifeguard working at a five-star resort near Tulum was gunned down. Mexican authorities were quick to insist that the violence took place away from the hotel zone. But it's been creeping out of the Mexican *barrios* and closer to tourist hot spots. I almost cancelled our flight until JoJo convinced me, as she always does.

"You're safe here, Rudy" she purred on FaceTime. "You've come three years in a row and the closest you've come to a drug cartel is a teenager smoking pot on the beach."

I wonder if I'll have to pay protection money to Foreign Fred. Fred isn't even his real name. I found out from Jimmy. It's Fiske. He changed it when he moved to Mexico to set up shop, leaving his international import/export business identity behind him in Norway.

Or *did* he?

I share these thoughts with Neil after we crawl, or rather stumble, into bed, long after Christopher and Elizabeth discreetly slipped away. They missed the sand show. Ricky passing out on the beach, a sauced and naked Moby Thick, harpooned by his own drunkenness; Al rescuing a wailing Sally from the undertow or "under toad" as she drunkenly put it, reminding me of Garp's young son, but he's got a legitimate excuse – he's a character in a John Irving novel; Brenda getting stung by a jellyfish; Foreign Fred firing off fireworks and scaring the locals; and, finally, Jimmy's tablet dying. Nothing left to drown out the sound of the vomiting.

"Fiske is not the leader of a drug cartel," Neil says, pulling off the sheets. "Besides, who ever heard of a Norwegian drug lord?"

"Exactly. What better cover. *And* he's got international connections."

"No, Rudy. You don't see Al Pacino or Johnny Depp doing bad Norwegian accents while snorting cocaine on screen. The only 'snow' Fiske is dealing with is the alpine skiing he left behind when he came here."

"What about that show *Lillehammer*?"

"Go to sleep."

I get up, wrestle with the doorknob, trip over Tortilla in the hallway, and find the kitchen faucet. I drink a gallon of water and pass out.

─╱╲─

KA-THWICK!

There is something on the roof. It sounds like a family of prehistoric raccoons. Everything is bigger in Mexico, including hangovers.

"Neil, wake up!" I jab him in the ribs.

"What?" he groans groggily.

"There's something on the roof. Something big."

KA-THWICK!

"That is big," he says, sitting up and staring up and beyond the ceiling fan.

"It's Foreign Fred!"

"It's not Foreign Fred."

"Or one his goons. He wants me dead because he knows I know."

"Will you relax? It's an animal of some kind. It's probably just a big lizard."

KA-THWICK!

If it is a lizard, then Godzilla is up on the roof.

A scrambling sound and then silence.

"See," he says. "No drug cartel hitman. Go to sleep." He rolls over and falls back to sleep. I hate that he can sleep through anything. A bomb could land in our back yard and he'd still wake up fresh and rested. Eventually I fall asleep, dreaming of giant lizard-people driving black SUVs, carrying machine guns, their trunks filled with bags of Columbian blow.

⟶⟨⟨⟶

"Ah, you heard Poncho Villa last night," Jimmy says over a breakfast of toast, peanut butter, and fried beans.

"Who?" I ask, giving Neil an "I told you so" look.

"Poncho Villa," repeats Jimmy.

"Pancho," interrupts Neil.

"Pancho is the revolutionary. Poncho is an iguana who lives in the neighbourhood. Big fella too. You'll most likely see him this afternoon. He loves to sun on that rock out there." He points to a rocky outcropping on the beach.

"See," says Neil. He turns to Jimmy. "He thinks Fred is a drug lord."

"I do not," I lie, spilling my coffee on my shorts.

Later that afternoon I read by the pool, enjoying a moment out of the midday sun with a bottle of water and a banana. I notice something appear from behind JoJo's makeshift clothesline. It is dull grey in colour with a tall dorsal crest. A large spiny iguana. He is huge, almost five feet long, half of which is his rough scaly tail. Poncho Villa, the iguana revolutionary, has arrived. He looks about, sees me mid-banana, and gradually noses his way toward me.

I stretch out my legs hoping to discourage him from coming any closer.

I start eating my banana faster.

He stares at me, a hungry purpose in his eyes.

I take another bite.

He swishes his tail.

I take another bite.

Poncho Villa lets out a low hiss.

I can't move. Paralyzed with lizard fear, my vocal cords freeze. I am going to die from a lizard attack on my reading week vacation. It isn't exactly what I envisioned for my obituary. "College teacher eaten by Mexican guerilla iguana."

I close my eyes, hold my breath, and stand (or rather sit) my ground. Suddenly two strong-clawed legs scrabble up mine. Disregarding the rules about not feeding wild animals, I throw the last of my banana on the stone patio floor next to Poncho Villa. He snatches it up, scurries across the tiles, climbs up the rock fence that encircles the *casa*, and jumps onto a low-hanging tree branch, disappearing into the foliage.

I am furious with my sister. She is the cause of Poncho Villa's bold behaviour. She's always feeding the raccoons at her trailer park and wants to open a hobby petting zoo, but Jimmy is allergic to llama spit. Recklessly feeding bananas to an iguana the size of a crocodile is pushing it.

I did breathe a little easier when I convinced myself that Poncho isn't really dangerous, just an opportunist. Still, I wish I had packed my coyote stick. I've heard that Costa Ricans sell tourists colourful forked iguana sticks for a handsome sum. It sounds like fake news. It's a clear act of animal cruelty and Costa Rica is renowned for its ecotourism, not iguana bashing. It has to be a hoax. But now, after my banana-snatching close call, I wonder if Costa Rica might actually be leading the field in iguana-deterrent weapons, and that Mexico has some catching up to do.

That evening the four of us go out to dinner at Fred's, the expat bar, not Foreign Fred's home. No one is invited to his house, according to JoJo. Fred's is a tacky cross between Rick's Café Americano and a Disneyesque version of *The Flintstones* for adults, serving snowbirds and locals alike. Fred's is all about chill and watching the world go by; the bar itself is modelled after a prehistoric Bedrock cartoon cave-tavern, a mixture of boulders and timbers under a thatched roof – all housed inside an actual cave. Monster cocktails, endless popcorn, booths shaped like Fred Flintstone's car, patio lanterns hanging from stalactites, the friendly serving staff dressed as Betty, Wilma, and the adolescent versions of Pebbles and Bamm-Bamm who remember our names from last year. They even know what we ordered. The tips at Fred's are substantial. Staff turn-over is practically non-existent.

A large sign out front announces, "You'll have a yabba dabba doo time!" *Flintstones* paraphernalia decorates the walls. Classic '60s bubblegum rock bops and bangs out of two large overhead speakers disguised as pterodactyls perched above a cramped dance floor. Cheesy, cozy, and crazy, and packed to the ribs.

The use of *Flintstones* imagery to attract the tourist trade also plays an important role in Foreign Fred's assertions of a "with it" and "good-humoured" guy identity.

Fred Flintstone was not a drug dealer. No better disguise than a beloved '60s cartoon character. But, to me, the link to the famous American comedy cartoon is an indication that Cerritos is not so remote as to not be linked up with the global network, satellite TV, and drug smuggling.

We get a table at the back and order a round of Great Gazoo green margaritas and a rib plate combo to share. Unsurprisingly, Fred's menu is strictly barbecue, its specialty a Barney Rubble rib-eyed steak, grilled over coals, much like Barney himself. When the ribs arrive, I find them too fatty and the sauce is mostly ketchup. The alcohol distracts from the sub-par cuisine. Gathering by the *gringos* that nightly pack the bar, the cheap booze works. Neil orders a Dino pulled-pork sand-wich that is surprisingly tender and actually tastes like pork.

The happy hour crowd parts and Foreign Fred emerges wearing a raggedy deep sky-blue necktie and a sleeveless orange and black spotted loin cloth with a torn hemline. He looks like the Hanna-Barbera version of an ageing Chippendale's male stripper. He slyly works the room, mingling with the regulars, briefly joining the bar flies for a quick shot of Mr. Slate tequila, flirting with the women, and ordering his staff to push the Wilma wings and whiskey. Any other human being would look ridiculous in a Fred Flintstone costume. Not Foreign Fred. He wears it like a modern-day Roman emperor.

He catches Jimmy's wave and sits down between Neil and me.

"Hola, amigos. Pasando un buen rato?"

"You bet," sings Jimmy. How much more can Jimmy fawn over this guy.

"Why don't you just ask for his autograph, Jimmy?" I say, blowing out a noisy breath.

"Lo siento?" Foreign Fred interjects, stealing one of my ribs. "You have a problem with how I run my bar, *Rude*-rigo?"

"No," I say huffily.

"Tu problema?"

"I don't have a problem."

"You don't have a problem," he repeats each word slowly.

"No, I don't have a problem." I start to sweat. It's not the heat.

"Luego?" he says, leaning in and pressing his elbows down firmly on the table, blocking my view of Neil.

"Leggo?" I respond curtly. Jimmy gives me a nasty look.

"Then what?" Foreign Fred speaks plainly.

"Nothing. Can we please drop this?"

"Ah, I see. 'Let go of my ego.' You're jealous of me."

"I am not."

"Oh, but you are, my Canadian friend." He looks over to Jimmy. "Your brother-in-law is wound up tighter than a boa constrictor hugging a monkey. He needs to learn how to chill. I should take him deep-sea fishing. *Nadar con los peces.*" Foreign Fred laughs loud and hard.

I am in a scene from a mob movie with Fred Flintstone. Swimming with the fishes. Just what I need. Murdered by the Nordic leader of a Mexican drug cartel.

"Una broma," says Foreign Fred, ordering me another a drink.

"He's joking," says JoJo, kicking my shin under the table.

"Chill," says Jimmy.

"Your drug cartel paranoia is no longer funny," says Neil. "The heat has fried your brain. Drink some water. You're dehydrated."

"Okay, okay, I'm sorry," I mutter, taking Neil's water glass. "Can we just get back to drinking green aliens?"

I feel humiliated and ready for bed.

Foreign Fred's tone and expression brighten. "I was talking to some Aussie girls I met on the street and I said, 'Have you *chicas jóvenes* checked out that Flintstones bar?' and they said, 'Oh, no, it's too American, too artificial.' They hadn't even been inside yet. I offered to buy them a round if they'd come in for one drink. Once they get in here, they have an entirely different experience. And why? Because it's in a cave," he laughs, "and very 'natural.' Look at them now." He points to the dance floor where four tanned young women are drunkenly twisting and shouting, many rounds later. *"La magia de una cueva."*

I want to sleep in a caye.

―᠊ᜭᜰ᠊

KA-THWICK!

Poncho Villa is at it again, right on schedule.

Every night since the day of our arrival, at precisely four in the morning, the sound of a banana-stealing monster-iguana clatters across the roof.

By day five, I am exhausted, barely able to keep my eyes open. To add insult to injury, Poncho Villa has started following me to the beach in hopes of banana treats. JoJo has created an environmental no-no. I half-expect the fishermen of Cerritos to show up outside the casa at night with pitchforks and lanterns.

Nevertheless, I am just as bad. I keep feeding him. Out of guilt and fear of the repercussions I'll face if I don't. Poncho Villa could easily be the muscle for Foreign Fred's drug cartel.

Heat exhaustion and sleep deprivation make your mind do strange things.

KA-THWICK!

It hits me.

I have not seen Foreign Fred and Poncho Villa in the same place at the same time.

It becomes clear, clear as the ocean, clear as the blue sky. Nothing has ever been this clear.

Foreign Fred is a lizard-person.

It all makes sense: his physical appearance and demeanour, his piercing crystal blue eyes, the blonde shaggy hair, and his bar that keeps the North Americans in Cerritos drunk so they remain mind-controlled under his magic cave spell. World dominance is Foreign Fred's goal, cocaine his means.

―〳〵―

Most of Cerritos is rural pasture enclosed by barbed wire fencing. Palm trees and the ocean make up the background. Cows, horses, and chickens wander the dirt roads. It is a pastoral paradise coupled with mounds of shit.

It is low tide, the following afternoon, as I sink my toes into the warm white sand. Little waterspouts form beside my toes. I have seen tiny crabs race erratically along the beach and retreat into holes, but this is different. It is as if the beach is a giant waterbed that sprung a leak, and then another, and another.

A wind begins to blow in off the ocean. Strange. It's the dry season. High winds come with the wet season. I wave to Neil to get out of the water. He waves back and ignores me.

I bury my unease in my beer and lean back in a plastic chair warped by the sun to give it a reclining effect. I purchase my lunch from a snack stand on the beach. The home-made tortilla chips heaped on the plate are perfect for dipping into the ceviche of fresh fish caught off the coast. It might well be the best fish I've ever tasted if it weren't for my mounting anxiety. The spicy hot peppers don't help.

I order another two-dollar *chelada*, a lager beer on the rocks – *Pacífico* is my favourite – with a liberal dose of lime juice on the rim. It hits the spot.

Ka-thwick!

The sound startles me. I look behind me. Too late.

For a split second I swear I see Poncho Villa in a pink golf shirt disappearing behind a boulder.

"Hola, Rudrigo," shouts a male voice instead. I twist my neck back around to see Foreign Fred striding across the sand toward me, his toes oblivious to the sand crabs. He plunks a beach towel down on the hot sand beside me and sits down.

"You can't cure an asshole," he says icily.

It's the moment of my death.

"I've got no sympathy for those who blame others, who take no responsibility for their actions," he says. He is biding his time, playing with me, stretching my murder out.

"I always clean up after myself," I reply, quickly sobering up.

"Not you. The cruise ship. It's docking in Cancun and those assholes are allowing it."

"Who is?" I notice a rip in Foreign Fred's pink golf shirt.

"The Mexican government. *Malditos pendejos.* The Norwegian cruise line isn't taking any responsibility. They're blaming the Chinese, claiming it was an infected passenger from Beijing who ate a fruit bat before boarding that started this mess. Can you believe it? And there are more cases. Over 50 now. Both crew and passengers. Just what I need, a flu bug to hit right in the middle of tourist season. *Maldito infierno.*"

His eyes could spit blood.

"And the *gringos* are oblivious," he continues in disgust. "Look at them."

I spy a group of teenagers playing beach volleyball, children digging in the sand, parents reading and dozing under large striped umbrellas, and Brenda baking in the heat. Now, there's a genuine lizard. Her scaly and dry skin is as brown as shoe leather.

Foreign Fred reaches into a mini-beach cooler and cracks open a Corona.

"Here's to the stupidity of mankind," he says with cold-blooded satisfaction, his mood shifting with the change in the wind's direction. He raises his beer and toasts the blazing sun. "Corona virus, here we come."

He grins eerily for a brief instant.

His teeth glisten.

His tongue flicks.

The lizard-people are about to make a move.

John Hart

A PORTRAIT OF THE ARTIST AS A YOUNG WOMAN

In 1910, a young Emily (Millie) Carr travelled to Paris to discover the New Art. She was accompanied by her sister Alice as chaperone.

Will the New Art help me to see anew? I have heard it liked, praised, revered. Also hated, ridiculed. Mere reproductions do not suffice, I need to see it for myself. My goal: to learn techniques to capture the rhythms of nature, the green turmoil of the forests of home, the majestic blue of the sky.

I hold my friend Sophie's letter of introduction in my hand as Alice directs us to the Seine and over to the Right Bank. Sophie, who studied here, who had showings in London, who made opportunity for herself until her mother called her home to marry the priest. The poor widower needed a new wife, the children needed a mother, so Sophie had to return. Back at home, she brought her charges to my barn and taught me to paint while the children played.

I simply wish to present Sophie's letter to her mentor, Mr. Harry Gibb, make an appointment, and leave behind a small portfolio of landscape sketches. Instead, we are ushered right in by Mrs. Gibb. We climb a steep, narrow staircase to the second floor, above a furniture shop. The stairs smell of wood, stain, turpentine; little swirls of sawdust dance in the corner of each tread as we pass.

In his studio, Mr. Gibb has fashioned a wooden trellis on which to hang his many paintings. They rise from the floor to the high ceiling in a blaze of colour. My first sight of the New Art! I stand staring in amazement, there are so many perplexities for me to sort out.

What rich, delicious juiciness in colours, vivid and intensified with complementary hues, a subtle interplay between warm and cool tones. Fluid, broad brushstrokes. A landscape of a grove of tall, thin trees in shadow, the tree trunks in apparent easy brushstrokes, a dappling of green, mere suggestions of leaves. Here, a brown barn, square and solid, but all around a playful wash of green and strokes of yellow, highlighted with pink, red, magenta, and royal blue even, flowers dotting the grassy field. Loose and free, suggestive rather than detailed, an effortless flow of energy.

His pictures rejoice!

Alice barely looks at the paintings. The Modern appalls her, which makes me like it that much more. She sits on the chesterfield to have tea with Mrs. Gibb.

I finish walking the length of the room. Mr. Gibb is watching me. He has remained silent the entire time, his mouth a crooked, tight-lipped twist. I do not wish to betray my ignorance by saying the wrong thing.

Relief, as he speaks first: "Show me your work."

"Oh yes, of course, Mr. Gibb," I say, and raise my portfolio. "I brought a few sketches, some of my—"

"Your work will stand for itself, yes? Let me look on my own," he says.

"Of course, sorry." I open the portfolio, hold it open in my palms, facing it toward him.

"Hm. Yes. Yes," he says, scanning through several sketches. He turns over another.

"This one is—" I begin.

"No need to explain."

"Sorry."

"Or apologize." Another. "You have an eye for representation," he says. "But it's rather inert. Where is the emotion?" He waves at me to close the portfolio. "I can see Sophie's influence."

"Yes, she—"

"Remarkable girl." He nods his chin at my portfolio and says, "It's formal, but shows promise, your work."

"Thank you, sir."

"Not at all, not at all. You've come to learn the New Art, haven't you?" He puts his hands in his pockets and looks toward his paintings.

"I was hoping you could tell me where—" I start.

"Colorossi," he talks over me.

"—to study. Colorossi? Not Julien's?"

"No, no, no, my dear girl." He chuckles and glances at Mrs. Gibb to see if she has heard, but she is still in conversation with Alice. "At Julien's the classes are separate. At Colorrosi's male and female students work together. It's better."

I nod in agreement.

"A distinct advantage for women students to see the stronger work of men."

"But—" I try to interject. Working alongside is different than being considered a level, or more, below.

"They'll try to put you on the fourth or fifth floor."

"Fourth or fifth, yes."

"No, don't let them," he says, turning to face me. "The top floors are reserved for amateurs. Women, of course. Insist on the second floor, if you can, third if they resist." He places his hand behind his back and the twist of tight smile returns. "Now, how is our dear Sophie?"

"Busy with her new family."

"What a shame."

⤙⤚

Infuriating! "'The work of men is stronger…'" I say as I march away, my anger propelling me forward.

"Mrs. Gibb was nice," Alice offers, following behind me.

Are we always considered weak? I carry my painting gear – three and a half stone! – into the forests and along the coasts!

"Absolutely galling, Alice."

"He seemed a bit gruff, but that was nice of him to – Millie, please, I can't keep up with you."

Men get approval. Exhibitions. Opportunities. Their painting is a vocation, not a hobby. They get time to study, develop. But they do not have a monopoly on paint or canvas. Or on seeing.

I turn a corner and almost walk into an old woman pulling a small cart. I veer sharply around her.

"Could you slow down?" Alice calls out.

I stop and turn around. "I'm not even allowed to travel alone!"

"What are you on about?" Alice says, as she comes near.

"I'm a grown woman. I can take care of myself. I had to work to make this happen, Alice."

"I know, Millie. You worked extremely hard."

I resume walking.

My eldest sister said I shouldn't come. The trustees of our parents' estate told me I couldn't come. But I gave art lessons and pottery classes to children and once I had earned enough, I booked my ticket. I defied them and chose my own path.

Alice runs up to me, takes hold of my arm and forces me to stop.

"Where do we need to race to?"

"The art school. I want to sign up."

"Did you get the address?"

"No." I wanted to leave quickly.

"So you're simply marching to who knows where?" She looks around.

"I'm not going back to ask him."

Alice stops to ask for directions from an older woman sitting at a flower stall. The woman explains with many gestures and Alice tries to repeat the semaphore.

"The Left Bank is back that way," Alice says, pointing behind us.

"We've been going the wrong way?" I bark at her. "Speak up, for goodness' sake!"

Alice tucks her arm in mine and leads me, at a calmer pace, toward the river.

"Absolutely galling!" I say again, thinking of Mr. Gibb's view of women painters, women students! He respected Sophie, though, until she married.

"Did he not say that you show promise?"

"Faint praise, Alice. Faint praise."

─╮╰─

Five francs per month for instruction and use of the studio, easels provided. Alice is practicing her French, though is speaking very slowly and deliberately to a languid young man who is slouching behind a counter in a tiny vestibule of an office.

She turns to me to say, "Fifth floor?"

"No, second or third," I tell her. She turns to the young man and I poke her in the back. "Be firm."

Alice waves her hand behind her to stop me from bothering her. When she finishes with the arrangements, she turns to say, "As you wish. Second floor. 2C."

I want to see the classroom before I start tomorrow so we follow some young men up the wide staircase to the second floor. The hallway is dim, warm, damp, and noisy with many people standing and chatting, or sitting on a row of benches pushed up against the wall. The students are gathered in groups, smoking, and speaking in several languages, though not an English word among them.

We make it to the end of the hallway but cannot find the studio. Alice gets a young woman's attention and discovers that my studio is on the third floor – the second storey. Up we go, up a narrower staircase, with the heat growing stronger still, the air thicker. My stomach seizes up with nerves and excitement.

My goal for three years and here I am, about to meet other painters also here to discover and attempt the New Art, ready to learn, to break free from the old traditions. People dedicated to painting as a craft, not merely a hobby.

The studio is third door down, with a dozen or so men at easels or in conversation. I'm struck by the smells of cigarettes, cigars, pipes, oil paints, paint thinners, perspiration, and unwashed clothing. There is dirt scattered on the floor from everyone's boots. Alice puts her sleeve to cover her mouth. I try to stifle a cough but the tiny noise draws attention to us. Several of the men look in our direction for a moment but they merely turn back to their activities, indifferent after the momentary interruption.

"There's your class," Alice says. She turns away and scurries back down the stairs. I remain a few moments longer, to consider the room, the men, the site where my learning will begin.

━ ⁄ ∖ ━

The next morning, Alice chaperones me back to the school but stays at the foot of the staircase. I go up alone and stop at the threshold of the classroom, a moment to allow myself to adjust to the heat, the smells, the low light.

Where might I squeeze myself quietly, unobtrusively into a corner, to set up? I skirt around the back of the class and put my sketch sheets on an empty easel in the back row. As I set my paint box down, I notice a gentleman across the room watching me, his hand and paintbrush suspended in the air. I look away, with the preoccupation of shifting my paint box a little.

On my right a young gentleman, dark hair falling around his downcast face, is very studiously sprinkling tobacco onto a square of paper. On my left, a man with short dark hair, olive skin, amply filling his clothes, is engaged in debate with the man on his other side. Aggressively whispering – in Italian? Greek? – faces flushed, sweat dripping from their brows, paint rags bunched in their large hands. I am opening my paint box when one claps his hand on the other's shoulder, they fall against each other laughing loudly. I smile, to acknowledge the jocularity, but they aren't including anyone else.

Back on my right, the glowing tobacco at the end of the young man's cigarette holds him transfixed. I shift back a little so I can catch a glimpse of his work – blank. Ah, he hasn't started yet. I smile in familiarity at the situation.

I turn back to my paint box and pretend to fiddle with the tubes and brushes inside while I glance around the room again.

Three loosely curved rows of easels, most of them occupied, all but mine by men. That man across the room is still looking at me. My eyes meet his yet again. I nod. No response from him – no curiosity or welcome or even anger. I raise my eyebrows a bit, my shoulders too. He moves his paintbrush slowly back down to his palette and shifts his gaze back to his own study.

Even on this pleasant September day, a stove in the far corner is in use. Gas lights overhead add to the warmth of the room. I wipe my forehead with one of my rags. The men all in light shirts, sleeves rolled up. I am overdressed in long sleeves and woolen skirt.

The forest of easels encircles a table covered with a dark cloth. A golden goblet, three books piled loosely on one another and three red apples.

When is the lesson to begin? Many of the students have started working on their own. Not my neighbour, though, whose cigarette is done but now the tips of his pencils are mesmerizing him. The talkers to my left are engaged in another rapid conversation.

As I look to the objects of still life, I can see the easel of the person in front of me. The man there, long dark hair falling around the collar of his dirtied white shirt, furiously scribbles and shades on his paper. A trio of apples already complete hovers at the top of his page, a new trio takes shape underneath. Shoulders hunched, back round, head forward, he peeks around the side of his easel to look at the subject before scrutinizing his work and attacking it once more.

No choice but to start. I adjust my stool, select a hard pencil and face my blank sheet.

I'll begin with the goblet – a horizontal concave line, like a hammock, then curving lines down either side, a line parallel to the top for the base. The Holy Grail, perhaps. Straight lines of

the books – the Good Word? The tempting apples, I create circles, shade in the left-hand sides, add a line for a stem on each.
Next the altar.

It's not working. I scratch over it all.

In front of me the Scribbler's back blocks my view of his
work. The Dreamer hasn't yet put pencil to paper. The Talkers
occasionally stab at their paper with far less intention and
energy than arguing a point with each other. The Starer is still
the only one to acknowledge me.

These are the men whose work I'll benefit from seeing?

~⁄ı∖~

Where to start? The idea, the sketch, the foreground. In this
foreground a young artist, newly arrived in Paris, sitting on the
sole chair in her apartment, easel in front of her turned toward
the window. The woman, come for the New Art, is alone – her
sister is out at market. A calm hush, conducive for work.

The sketch – a proposal of what's to come. What is the subject, how is it framed? A guide to lay out point of view, perspective, scale. The sketch should not dwell in detail, but broad
strokes, feeling, expression. Loose, spontaneous. Qualities she's
never had. How belaboured her efforts were before! A vase of
flowers, each stem, flower, even individual petal, delineated in
exact detail. A photograph can do that now, a threat to an
artist's interpretation or the botanist's drawing.

The young woman as a girl – her father was a botanist, an
amateur to be certain, yet with a keen eye. He enjoyed delving
into forests and fields, collecting samples, bringing them home
to examine. She watched as he needed only paper, pencil, and
fine attention to detail to create a wonderful likeness. She
adored him then, wanted to emulate him.

His study was his private domain where he continued his business affairs in the evening before turning to his hobby. A small room, lined with dark oak and shelves of books. A richly stained cherry wood desk, a green blotter, and neat piles of papers, ledgers, and botanical books.

One night I stood in the shadows of the hallway, holding my breath. He didn't look up but must have sensed my presence and simply waved me forward. I stepped in as quietly as I could, paper and pencil in hand. He beckoned again, I scooted to sit down beside his desk where I could share the circle of yellow light that emanated from the oil lamp.

I rested my paper on my knees; he handed me a specimen of bigleaf maple. I spent that first evening scratching at the paper, making distorted reproductions of the lobed leaf, its striations and veins and wavy teeth. I was completely absorbed until Father said, Get along now before they think you've run away again. I scrambled to stand and headed for the door but, without taking his eyes from his ledger, he said, Leave your paper so I can see what you've done. I returned to the desk, hesitated a moment, then gently laid the paper face down before I fled from the room.

Now here: a Parisian courtyard, shrubbery, flowering vines climbing the brick walls. The window, slightly ajar, a frame for the view outside. Start with this.

※

Each day the trinity at the front of the class – the books, apples and wine goblet – are in a new position. The students, on the other hand, have mostly stationed themselves at their familiar easels, as I myself have done.

Beside me the Dreamer, transfixed by everything except painting; behind, the Conductor, arms like windmills in their grand sweeping gestures; and altogether too close to a Talker, only the one here today. These fellows have various degrees of discipline: some are productive, others not so much. Then again, I have only been idly sketching thus far today.

My time in class has been silent, my only conversations are with Alice, who dutifully returns at lunchtime with some bread and cheese for me, and today some crisp, crunchy wax beans from the market. No doubt it would be useful to know the language, but I'm here for the art.

The instructor has still not come. This morning I made Alice speak to the languorous youth at the front desk who said that the instructors only visit a couple of times a week.

Behold, early afternoon, a man strides in, a hush falls, the students put down their pencils or brushes. He starts in the far corner, speaking to a dark-haired young man there. As he moves from easel to easel, I study him. His head throws out strands of grey hair in every direction, even though a black ribbon is pulled tight at the back; the top and the sides go unbound and unchecked. His wire spectacles rest on his large, red nose. Skin, mottled; his pants, loose; his sweater, much too large for him. He has a slight limp or discomfort in his right leg; he jerks a bit as he walks, each stride slow, deliberate.

I wait nervously for my first meeting, the critique he will offer. It is hard to breathe, with the smoke and stale air in the room. Again the stove belches out black smoke. Mysterious, when I never see anyone tend it.

Everyone awaits his turn. The solo Talker is uncharacteristically silent and somewhat gloomy. The Dreamer runs his fingers along the sides of his sketch papers, up one side, across the top, down the other. He's wearing a tweed newsboy cap, a scarf loosely wrapped around his neck. Over his shirt a vest, an ill-fitting sweater, dark wool pants. I want to shed some layers of clothing, and this boy has more than necessary? Truly his head is not attached well to the rest of him.

The instructor steps closer, contemplates the sketch of the Talker for a moment and comments. His back is to me, I cannot hear what he is saying, even if I could understand. The Talker says something, the instructor laughs, a phlegmy, throaty laugh. Now the mood is genial, more talking and laughing follow. I try to anticipate when their conversation will end. The instructor begins to turn, the Talker says something more, yet more discussion.

Finally the instructor claps the Talker on the back with one more chuckle that ends with a sigh, like a final release of a bellow. He turns to me. I sit a bit straighter. The instructor's eyes go to my drawing first then quickly to my person, eyebrows raised. He looks me down before returning his gaze to the work. He mumbles a few words. I say, "English. Please." He continues mumbling. He points at my work a couple of times, poking at an apple, traces his fingers along an outside curve before pointing to the objects at the front of the room. He clasps his hands behind his back and steps over to the Dreamer.

That is all? I need more. I need instruction. Insight. Is there no one in class to translate? I need Alice.

I make my way around the forum of easels to the door. In the hallway, I push through the clusters of talkers and smokers. Down, down, down the main staircase into the lobby but I can't spot Alice. Light streams in through the open front door, a beacon to draw me there. Perhaps she is outside. I need her before the instructor disappears, perhaps not to return for days more.

I step out and scan the street to see if Alice is approaching. Where is she?

I lean against the building to wait for her, to avoid the choking air inside and this stupid situation I've put myself in. The clouds are low and grey, a screen of soot hangs in the sky, stinging my eyes.

━✦━

I can't let this discourage me – and I've paid for the month – so I must return. I climb the stairs, re-enter the room. The instructor is no longer here, the men have resumed their work. As usual, no one acknowledges my presence or speaks to me. Nary an encouragement, a suggestion or a sympathetic word.

I spend the rest of the afternoon tense and anxious, in vain attempts to work. I'm only sketching half-heartedly, an effort to accomplish something.

As I come down the stairs at the end of the day, I spot Alice sitting on a narrow couch tucked in a dim corner. A book on Paris and her little notebook in her lap, but she is watching the students as they come and go. She stands up when she spies me.

"You weren't here earlier, Alice." I speak more harshly than I intend.

"No, I went to sit in the churchyard nearby."

"The instructor came this afternoon."

"Oh, Millie, you came down to look for me? I'm sorry I wasn't here for you."

"The day is done, Alice. Let's go home."

An unexpected need for her companionship, my vexation melts. It's a comfort to find her in the lobby. Alice gathers her books and we step outside.

"Truth be told, he didn't actually say much," I offer, as we start walking.

"Still, you've been waiting for him. Next time, Millie, I'll stay here so this doesn't happen again."

She doesn't hold my sharpness against me or she's hiding it well.

"Thank you, Alice," I say, then to engage her I ask, "What have you been reading about?"

"The electric lights that replaced the gas lamps. And that most of the buildings are made from limestone quarried from under the city," she tells me as we make our way up the street.

She points into a bakery. I let her go in by herself to avoid being asked anything in French. Alice steps out of the shop, baguette in hand, and resumes her cheery talk. She seems to need my company as well.

The street sweepers are out, cleaning with their twiggy brooms. The Chinese launderer at the head of our street is standing in his store door; he bows as we pass him. A beggar woman sits silent sentry on our corner, head covered in a dark, dirty shawl that she folds her hands into and hugs to her body. I ask Alice for a coin which I put in the metal cup at the woman's feet. She offers me a pencil from within her shawl. I reach out to take it.

―✳―

"Diana the Huntress," Alice announces, reading from her guidebook, naming the statue of this woman, barely clothed, her right hand resting on a greyhound on her right. I prefer the statue we passed earlier, "Diana with a Doe." In that one, at least, she was clothed. Her left hand held on to a springing doe beside her, her right was reaching back into a quiver of arrows strung over her shoulder. She was more active, more practical, not merely on display. Alice gazes at Diana the Huntress for a few moments more before nodding and we move on.

With each step, our shoes make a small crunch on the loose gravel of the well-ordered pathways of the Tuileries. We stroll a grand pedestrian avenue away from the Louvre palace, the river to our left. I must give Alice this outing together, to mollify her. And this garden visit will inspire me with nature, she says, so she feels she's doing me a favour.

Out for a Sunday stroll like the couples, the young men and women in pairs or trios, small parties of women, mothers or governesses with prams doing a round or two of the grounds. People on parade, not taking exercise, like I prefer, or here to appreciate wildlife. As Alice says, however, it is still pleasant to be outdoors. The light of the day is diffused under the low clouds. And we both like to observe the people and places about us.

Chairs are scattered around the garden, all occupied. Benches line the reflecting pools of the gardens. Amongst the regimented rows of low bushes, evenly spaced in diamond patterns surrounding the sunken octagonal basin of water, people are sitting or lying on the grass.

Alice leads us to a free spot and we alight. She settles herself on the grass, tucks her legs under her, arranges her skirts, puts her book on her lap. I flump down, sit cross-legged, lay my sketch pad in front of me.

"A royal palace was here," Alice tells me. She taps the cover of her guidebook. "Mr. Baedeker says it burned down a number of years ago and was demolished only recently. And now we're here, sitting on all this history."

"Well, I'm trying to get a bit more comfortable on all this history," I say, shifting over a smidgen because of a lump in the lawn.

"Think of all the royal pomp and pageantry that used to be here!"

"What else is in your guidebook?" I ask, hoping she'll open the book straight away.

"Are you going to sketch?"

I smooth out the open page of my notebook as my response.

"I can read aloud to you," she offers.

Head down, I hum aloud.

"Oh, you're exasperating!" she laughs.

The reflecting pools stretch out on either side of the garden paths, lined by asters. Deep rich crimson blooms atop teeming green stalks. I long to transcribe one in detail, a botanist's sketch. But instead I need to see anew, to capture the quantity of flowers in a broader way, in the new style.

I start with the long rectangles of dark water from our side angle first, the further end narrowing in proper perspective. From the closest corner, I begin to add the flowers, a jumble of stalks and leaves, topped with the ruffled circles of the flower heads.

I glance at Alice who is making a show of turning a page in her book, though she is looking toward the palace.

I look down to my page. Everything is too precise – the lines, the volume, the detail. Around me, the gardens, hedges and lawns of the Tuileries are laid out so carefully and geometrically, tamed, with little left to nature. A different beauty, the French way, disciplined. I prefer my wild gardens, the tangled, haphazard style of our flowers, grasses and bushes jostling together.

Abandon rigidity! Let disorder rule!

The New Art foregoes detail. I need to see differently, to try harder. I need to start again.

I turn the page. My right hand glides across the rough sketch paper, fingertips skimming the surface from the spine to the notebook's edge. The blank page, white and waiting, available should inspiration present itself.

—⁊⥃⟨⟩⥄⇍—

Three of Alice's guidebooks stacked neatly on our table, three tin paint tubes, a small brass candlestick holder and short lit candle. I've had to arrange these and rearrange them. So silly, the false naturalness of their composition belies any happenstance.

Here I sit, equally as awkward. What am I supposed to see? What do I need to capture?

I abandon the still life for a moment – a quick sketch will get me started. A small circle, near the top left of the page, scratching with the pencil to fill it in. More scratching forward, downward, sideways, to complete my hair. My nose in profile, the lips, the chin, the neck. A curve for my high collar, another for my back, then the sleeve. I sit flat. I draw the straight back of the chair, a straight line too for the seat. My long skirt hiding my legs, and small boots. I fill my clothes in, without detail.

I haven't yet filled in the eyes. Nor the hands.

Nor anything else to the right. There I sit in the caricature, gazing unseeing, at the blank space beside me. It's not nothing; rather it's not something yet.

Father didn't lack confidence, curiosity, or initiative. He plunged ahead and took chances. How far he travelled! How hard he worked! A merchant, a botanist by hobby and an adventurer too. He escaped the tradition and predictability of his homeland and went to California. Not lured by gold, like many others, but to sell supplies to those who sought far-fetched bonanzas. More stable than risking everything on a claim that might come to naught. With modest wealth he returned home, looking to establish himself, but was still unhappy. Again he left the old country, this time with a wife, and returned to the new world. A renewed beginning.

He acquired a large tract of land on Vancouver Island, built a house for his wife and a growing brood of daughters. A house made of stone with a formal parlour and dining room, a study for himself, a back kitchen, a second floor of bedrooms. They planted orchards out back, meadows of grass and wildflowers. He established a park at the farthest end of the property to maintain full access to nature and the ocean beyond.

With great interest, Father set out to discover new species in the new world. Mother, hoping I'd expend my interminable energy, sent me with him on his long walks. We hiked through the grass, the tall brush, the rocklands, the sweep of the meadow to the cliff to the sea. He pointed out the red pines that crowned the high point of the park, the arbutus trees that dipped their branches into the ocean.

We collected leaves and fronds, studied roots, stems, foliage. Then Father put them carefully into his leather satchel to take home. We marvelled at the heights of the various trees and their barks, distinguishing between deciduous and coniferous, leaves and needles. A new world of flora – lady fern, ox-eye daisy, stinging nettle, flowers from the salal bush.

At home, we spent many a night in peaceful solitude, pencils working away on yellow paper, meticulously translating the specimens we collected on that day's walk. A leaf, a blade of grass, a flower laid flat, a stalk split open. Look at the size, shape, lines, texture. Look again. Look closer. My first efforts were sloppy. He pushed me, always encouraging in his brusque manner.

Sometimes we'd ride our horses further inland to the great soaring forests, the canopy high above us. The Douglas fir with its flat pointed tips of needles, the distinctive yellowish groove, the papery scales of its cones. The red cedar with drooping branches turned up at the tips and small egg-like cones. Grand trunks that we could live in if hollowed, moss and lichen underfoot, and a spread of ferns. The air was moist and clean, the ground soft and welcoming. Sketchpads in satchels, we also took tea with us and set up stools to sit and draw.

In the harsher weather, we retired to his study. I sat on the woven Oriental carpet that had travelled all the miles of his journeys with him. My sisters had their kitchen, my brother made forts under the dining-room table, my mother was always lying in the parlour, but Father and I had his study.

He taught me diligence, observation, detail. He taught me about nature, its intricacies in each and every specimen. He let me sit astride my horse instead of side-saddle, as ladies were expected.

I want to ride out into the forest or walk along the beach. I want my hand to comb through the grasses as I walk toward the park. Those moments of beauty and wonder I aim to capture in my work. The majesty of the natural world, the idea of freedom and expansiveness.

That's what I want to capture, but instead I am confined to a classroom, exercises I don't understand, inanimate objects like those still in front of me. What if this wasn't the right journey to undertake?

⁓

I've let Alice persuade me to come to the Luxembourg Gardens to visit more nature. Rows of low hedges line the walking paths, straight and neat, symmetrical in their forced patterns. Flowerbeds are strictly delineated. But oh, the flowers within are lush and ripe, a final crescendo in autumn as they rush toward rot and frost, a last gasp of bursting beauty. White roses and auburn asters, scattered with monkshood and Echinacea blooms.

As we stroll, we pass an apiary, tennis and bowling lawns, a children's puppet theatre. A performance is happening for the children gathered on the ground, merry little hedgehogs they, curled and rolling in laughter.

Alice leads me to a fountain she read about in one of her books. There is a long rectangular pool lined with a small fence decorated with urns along the whole perimeter. At the far end an arched portico with a large bronze statue of a man perched on a rock to look below him at a couple carved from milk-white marble, caught in a lovers' embrace.

"Can you see the trick?" Alice asks.

The water appears on an angle, like it should be running down to the portico but instead it is still. How clever: the horizon is raised at the back to make it look like the pool is tilted. A forced perspective, so our eyes make it seem like the water isn't level.

It's a pleasant temperature, especially for September. Much nicer, just as Alice suggested it would be, than the confines of our lodging or the dimness of class and its choking smoke-filled air. The clouds are lighter and higher today, I assume on account of the factories being closed for the day of rest.

There are many people milling about – couples, families, domestics, the newspaper hawker, the ice seller; ladies and soldiers, lingerers and strollers, preeners and leaners. Chess players, backs rounded from age, huddle over boards in pairs of parentheses.

Alice buys a newspaper. "More to practice my reading than for information," she tells me. "There are so many words I don't yet know."

"Most likely they're particular to the dialect here or colloquialisms," I say. "I know you'll persist."

"I could teach you a few words, if you'd like."

"I'm here—" I begin, but Alice interrupts.

"For the art, I know, Millie. But a few pleasantries—?"

"I have neither the ear nor the patience," I say firmly.

"For pleasantries in either language?" Alice asks with a sly grin.

She secures a chair for me under a big plane tree and goes off to find one for herself. It's a very fragile chair: for the seat, only three small slats of wood, painted green, over the tiniest threads of metal that keep the chair upright, and one slat on which to rest my back. The feet of this flimsy contraption are settled into the loose pebbles spread underfoot in this section of the park. Not the most comfortable of chairs; even so, they seem to be at a premium. In the scattering of shade-sitters, the gentleman closest to me, with white hair and a loose frayed suit, rests his chin on his chest as he snores lightly.

Small sketch pad on my knee, I smooth out the top sheet and survey the scene – the raised basin of an octagonal fountain where children sail toy boats rented from a striped cabana. With their tall white triangular sails, the boats drift across the water, like ships in a large bay. Peaceful and tranquil, this harbour in miniature.

I'm surprised by a boy who comes to stand beside me. He is slight, not even as high as my shoulder. No hat on his head, dark hair tousled and unkempt, shirt and trousers worn and dull. His skin ruddy and touched by the summer sun, face dusted with freckles and framed by his protuberant ears. He holds a small stick in his left hand. Down-at-heel, but curious, energetic. There's no sign of anyone looking for him or minding him.

He asks something, in French, of course, but I can only offer a baffled smile. I look around quickly for Alice – she'd be able to discover his intentions. The boy gestures at my paper so I turn the pad toward him. He points to it again then at the basin. I don't wish to relinquish the pad to him entirely.

The boy puts out his hands, palms up, pulling toward himself and points once more at the basin. I offer him my pencil but he waves it away. He holds up one finger, then slips it under the top page. He raises his eyes to mine, gives a little nod. I nod back. He extracts the sheet and smiles once the paper is free.

Stick tucked under his arm, he kneels down to start folding and bending the paper this way and that. Folds, creases, turns, folds and creases the other side. Tongue tucked in the corner of his lips, he flips the paper over, bends some more, tucks some corners. He's made himself a boat. Only a small boat, but one with a bow and stern and a peak in the middle. It's nowhere near as tall as the elegant sailboats lazily drifting in the water, but he proudly holds it up for my inspection.

He darts away, bare feet skipping over the pebbles, heading to the fountain's pond. He leans against the stone lip, gently places his boat on the surface of the water, and blows. His boat sails slowly toward open water.

What joy, what simplicity – a piece of paper and a boy's imagination.

Alice returns with a chair of her own and settles herself, grumbling about being asked to pay for it. I watch the boy move around the edge of the pond as his paper boat bobs along, bumped by the rented yachts, the little ugly duckling amongst the swans.

His boat drifts to the edge, gets stuck against the stone lip. But the boy can't easily reach it, neither with hand or stick, not decorously, around a man and his daughter. She's in a little sailor dress and hat, each bright and shining white trimmed with navy blue, blonde hair hanging in curls down her back. The father is bent over impatiently explaining something to the girl, who keeps reaching for her boat. The father holds up his hand, the girl stomps one of her shining black shoes on the ground. The boy tries to maneuver again around the father and the petulant girl. The father yanks the sailboat from the water, uses his other hand to grab the girl's arm and pull her away. The boy rushes to his paper craft and nudges it away from the edge.

The toyman who lets the boats, a man with dark hair and a large moustache, puts down his newspaper to take back the sailboat from the father and daughter. Then he surveys the pond, reaches into the cabana and pulls out a large net on a stick. He takes long, purposeful strides toward the boy. I stand up quickly, my notepad falls to the ground.

"Millie, you seem alarmed."

"That toyman – he's going to – the boy—"

"Which boy, Millie?"

The boy too notices the toyman and reaches in quick to pluck out his boat. He gives it a little shake. He turns toward me, his soggy toy held delicately in his hand. The toyman is almost upon him but the boy's face breaks out into a big smile. He waves excitedly at me; I raise my hand to wave back but he has already dashed into the crowd and out of sight.

"He's gone now. Everything is perfectly all right," I say, as I pick up my sketch pad and sit back down. I lay the pad on my lap and think of the boy's creativity.

That's what I need – to go back to the beginning, the child-like wonder, to start anew. Learn a new vocabulary, like Alice is doing with her French. Build up new techniques. A new vision and approach.

Father taught me to be exact, to create a detailed likeness; my work so far has been careful, controlled, inert as Mr. Gibb said. Perspective, shape, volume, naturalness – how do I unlearn everything that I have been taught?

Here we are in Paris, for the New Art, and the freedom to explore. I worked hard to get here. This is my adventure, my new beginning. Anything is possible.

I glide my fingers across the paper as I look back to the fountain and scan briefly for the boy.

What will I do with my imagination today?

Jacob Gilligan

HAIL TO
THE ROACHES!

The crown weighed heavily upon my head despite its shifting.
And no, not a figurative crown; an actual solid ring of jewels
snug upon it, which had been directly responsible for a lifetime
of back pain. Yet I wore it. A deranged sense of pride? Have I
lost sense completely? More than likely. Even the clothes now
in rags had been rumoured to have been stitched by the angels
themselves. Nothing but tatters, barely hanging to my ailing
body, cloaked my shame. I'm sure that the exposure of a couple
of rib cages would surely ignite concern upon anyone I would
have encountered. There laid the biggest of problems. There
was nobody else. I could attempt a proper explanation exactly
why everyone was gone, but I will spare you such a depressing
monologue. The fact remained that this world was solely occupied by my inhabitants, the dust and sand. It found itself everywhere. Not one place did it occupy with my consent. Even the
jumble-slug that was in my mind turned it into a concrete
block. I dared to acknowledge the pressure my head held.
Enough to produce diamonds with enough time, which is all
I'd ever have left: time. My face, wrinkled with the trenches
which gathered the particles that welled up around my eyes,
as I looked out beyond a horizon so sharp that it hurt. The
reflection of the sun drove over a solid mass of colour that
blinded me, the sand white as snow sprayed a vivid burn across

the bottom half of my sight. A cloudless blue sky was all that remained in the negative space. Very much a rarity those days. However, this was not your regular blue sky. Something sat in it, like a purplish-green hue like the haze of gasoline binding together in a pothole along a desolate highway, as many I've come across. It held a poison mist that hovered along the inside of the earth's atmosphere. This would explain the desert of a once habitable paradise that, triumphant in its spectacular vision of might, would be buried by time and war. War so savage that not once the ancients spoke of such a mass extinction event in their grand battles of courage and adventure. What I witnessed in those days of long before will not soon remove themselves from my cooked head. The heat burnt the crown I wore into my scalp. It had left a ring of scabbing like a halo, but still, I did not remove it from my head. I let it fry itself into me. It's what I deserved and how I will see out the rest of my days.

I did not look for death. I did whatever it took to avoid him. Sometimes I saw him, peeking around the corner from the rubble of a café; or while I walked, I could hear him sneaking behind me. His footsteps now and then tapped a bit of debris, but every time I'd turn around, there was no one. I even found myself hiding from him. Sometimes all there was between me and him was a small, frayed wasteland cloth, and yet as much as he was persistent, I was resistant to his desire to take me. Why would one want to preserve himself in such a place? All that remained of my former self was but a broken shell. Boredom had become my only friend. It's with me wherever I might have found myself. All land had lost titles and all paths unique to others had vanished. Adapted to the wastes of former pine forests and tundras of frosted tip mountains. I rummaged through the litter of rusted irons and stainless steels hidden underneath a thin veil of soot, like beach toys scattered beneath the surface of a beach the tide had hidden. I emerged from my makeshift shelter, a hole dug with the nubs of fingers covered with the disintegrated husk of a wheelbarrow, waking before the sun had peeked over the horizon and cooked me inside my temporary home. The wind had settled from the night's temperature drop, but I was still blinded as the particles began pocketing themselves around my eyelids. I had spent the day in search of what little water may have managed to linger in the vast channel that had once been called the Mississippi. Some days are luckier than others for finding water. The congregation of anorexic animals shivering at the joints as they bend to drink from shallow pits of contaminated water was the best way to flag a location's drinkable sustenance. With my crooked black fire poker in hand, I'd charged at the group of weak animals too distracted by the will to survive. The doe I'd had my eye on hardly noticed my iron had penetrated its skeletal body right to the other side. All the other animals fled while the doe flailed and convulsed, pinned to the earth next to the mud hole. I pulled my dull blade out from my weathered satchel as I struggled against the thrashing deer. I pressed the blade into the animal's soft skull, ridding it of the pain of life as it foamed at the mouth. I looked around as the animals that had scattered remained a stone's throw away from the pit, watching and waiting for their turn. I drew from the bag a tiny, beaten-up canteen and pressed it down into the oily fluid and mud. As the bottle filled, I returned my focus to the deer and dragged it a few feet away from the pit, which spurred the other creatures to creep closer, despite the carnivorous human preparing a fresh kill. I removed the patchy pelt from the doe, exposing its stringy meat that clung to its fragile bones. I had nearly begun to chew on it like a dog before remembering what it meant if I had. Poisoning myself would only result in my death out here, so I hauled the kill out of the trench and set up camp next to a dilapidated body of a car partially submerged in the sand. I built myself a fire with haste as the sun started to rise. I poured the water into a small pot and some onto the end of a stick I had wrapped in cloth. I lit a match from a collection of matchbooks I had picked up along my travels and instantly the cloth was set aflame. I stuck it into the bundle of twigs and branches which ignited. With the water coming to a boil, I poured it back into my canteen and tossed the pot to the side. I then started stripping the meat away from the dead animal's bones. I skewered the bits of meat along the spit, bunched them up, leaving no room for exposed iron, to cook as much of it as I could. I wrapped myself in a sheet in preparation for the midday's bombardment of ultraviolent rays that had already done unfathomable damage to my skin. I drank some of the boiled water and nearly puked at the taste of it. As I waited, I watched the smaller animals in the ravine scurry around the dried-up pit. They fought and hissed at each other as to who would get the remaining water, but it wasn't long before they had given up on its potential and wandered off to go find another just like it. But there wasn't. By the time the meat had cooked I had drifted off. I slept until the sun's heat woke me to the unfortunate sight of the meat, partially burnt to a crisp on the skewer, which had fallen over into the ash. My heart jumped and then sank as I panicked, trying to pull out the meat with my bare hands. They sizzled against the scalding iron. So hungry I was that I had ignored the immense pain of the scorching skewer I held as I tore into the meat that remained. As I finished eating all there was that had remained edible, a glance toward the carcass sent me into a stint of depression I had not had the privilege to feel for some time. Swarms of maggots, larvae, and insects of all shapes and sizes had found my kill. I tore away strips of fabric from my blanket and wrapped them delicately around my hands to bandage them.

That night, as I slept in my shelter underneath the decrepit vehicle, tornados swept through the valley. I awoke to the hills on fire and decided it was time to move on. Everything that had been there the day prior was now gone, tossed about and scattered across the barren wastes and now buried underneath the sand. Maneuvering my wheelbarrow through the soft dirt demanded precision on my part. The blanket I wrapped around myself kept the sting of the sandstorm from pelting my skin, and the sunglasses I had removed from the corpses that littered my surroundings kept my sight intact, despite the density of the dust clouds that formed into a giant destructive colossus. I held tightly onto the crown, and that helped keep my blanket from taking off with the wind. I found myself unwittingly stumbling around the wreck of what was probably a small town as my heel collapsed into the fragile skull just in front of the broken welcoming sign. The horizon's jagged structures barely poked through the dunes. I marched between them, down the parted hills formed by way of the paved streets, where I passed an untold number of bones the winds had gathered in mass quantities. I was not entirely certain of where I would find myself, and then I came across a tiny house, miraculously undamaged despite the desolation of the neighbourhood. I left my wheelbarrow at the entrance of the broken white picket fencing, from which the gate had long since been torn away. I squeezed through the door, only slightly stuck open by the build-up sand at its base, into a shaded room. Inside, the house was untouched, a well-kept home in its pre-war condition, despite being covered in a thick layer of filth in all corners. The windows had been stained with fade and years worth of smudging that blocked out most of the day. The breeze which cut through the house compelled the structure to moan and creak in counterpoint to the muffled ambience of the outside hell. Pictures remained on the wall and dishes sat in the sink, still marked up with the last meal enjoyed by the original occupants. Magnets once stuck to the refrigerator had long ago fallen off and curled up in front of the door. I tried flicking on the light out of sheer habit. The light bulb in the fixture was broken and the fins attached to the fan were splintered and still. I stepped into the living room, where I was met with two perfectly preserved corpses at a small table, sitting casually in rocking chairs facing the television set. My first instinct was to back away in case they had noticed my presence. I leaned back into the room and I just stood there, looking at the empty sockets in their heads. Back in the kitchen, I raided their cupboards, finding only miscellaneous canned wet cat food and a bag of dry cat food. As the sun began to set, I broke one of the windows in the living room to exhaust the smoke from the fire I had built in the middle of their spacious floor. I placed one of the opened cans over top of the fire on a grate and cooked the preserved meat. I sat on the floor against the wall right across from the dead couple, still dressed in their best. The once happy colours in their clothes had long since faded to saturation that more resembled their surroundings. The fluid in the oval can began to bubble. I put on the oven mitts from the kitchen over top of my bandaged hands, removed the can from the fire, and placed it on the TV stand to cool a bit. My throat was void of all moisture; my tongue swelled at the base and cracked open like dry fruit, which I tried to cure by drinking from my canteen. I looked over to the bodies again, specifically towards the tuxedoed man with his jaw hanging loose from the rest of his skull and his hands still gripping the arms of his chair. I raised my canteen to him as if to toast.

"To Life," I declared, before taking another swig. I shoved a spoon into the can and began to eat. From inside the floor vent, a rather large cockroach poked its antennae out from the grille of the metal casing, feeling out its surroundings before it emerged from the safety of its hiding place. It scurried across the floor right up to the fire pit, where it stood still facing toward me for what felt like several minutes before it crawled over to the foot of the corpse. The insect climbed up the tailored pant leg into the creases of the jacket, then ascended, travelling up around the cervical vertebrae into the skull, where it sat in the opened mouth.

That night, the dreams were the same as always, the circumstances that led up to the present replayed. The screaming, the hysteria, the blood-curdling cries for mercy as my neighbours endured untold suffering – all of which I had missed and had to be left to the imagination as I trembled in the corner of a compact, heavily supplied room behind a fortified door. The persistent banging against the steel door that bled into my dream was manufactured by the blustery air blowing against a bent road sign upon the hood of a car. I rolled over onto my side against the wall, pushing the blankets off me as I wiped away the cold sweat from my brow. The fire had burned out, except for the ambers smouldering underneath the charred wood.

I sat up and began to mosey around the home in a tired-eyed daze, unable to return to my sleep, for fear of nightmares. I found my way up the stairs, which cracked and stressed underneath my feet. Despite the dark, I maneuvered through the house as if I knew what was beyond each door and in every corner. The layout was domestically familiar to me, everything in its right place. I opened the door to the master bedroom; the hinges whined as I stepped inside. The bed had been made and the drapes closed. The dressers were caked with dust and filled with folded, untouched clothes. In the corner next to the sliding door closet stood a tall floor mirror. The image was filthy, stained with sediment. I approached it, scared of the person who'd look back, no longer recognizable as myself, now a frail man deprived of fat. The thin muscles that hugged tightly against my bones hardly provided any shape to my being. My eyes had shrunk and my hair was longer than I've ever had it. The hunch in my back had worsened and my neck had begun to buckle and warp under the crown's precious elements. Still, the head apparel looked exquisite on me, despite the irregulates in my depiction. I picked up the framed photograph on the bedside table. In it, an old couple posed along the shore of a beach in their bathing suits, their ankles submerged in the surf. The old man still maintained a youthful, buff physique and wore his mustache proud and strong, while his companion shared in his youthful appearance, wearing a yellow polka-dot bikini with a large, buttoned shirt catching the ocean breeze, as her hand held down the sunhat about to lift off from her head. I admired the photo as I sat down on the edge of the bed, kicking up dust as my ass sank into the spread. I began to cough violently as the particles entered my lungs. I spat up thick phlegm as dark as the rug it landed on in front of me. Before I could catch my breath, something caught in my ears that forced me to muffle my gags. Faint sobs came from beyond the opened door. I remained still, trying to focus on the unmistakable blubbering of somebody's grief. I sat up from the bed gently to not let the springs groan.

I poked my head out into the hallway; the cries had become more pronounced, coming from downstairs. I snuck to the top of the stairs and stood, listening for a moment, before proceeding down. With each step I froze briefly, anticipating the cries would stop once whoever they were coming from grew wise to my presence. A couple of feet away from the dim ambers, the tuxedoed corpse buried his head in his bony hands. I looked to my left and my right with a twist on my face, unable to believe the sight in front of me. I approached the weeping corpse, assured of my present sleeping status. Without fear, I knelt in front of the fire, placed a couple more pieces of dried-out timber into the ambers as I stoked more flames from it with my poker. The dead man continued to cry. I cleared my throat loudly but still could not break his sorrow.

"What's the matter?" my gravelly, unused voice asked. Suddenly the corpse's head rose from his hands and looked over at me with his shallow, empty eye sockets.

"My wife… she's dead," the dead man said, his broken jaw slapping against his incisors, speaking in broken English. I looked over at the corpse sitting opposite him, bent and draped over in the chair.

"She is," I told him. "I'm sorry."

"We have to bury her," he said almost immediately.

"Right now?" I asked, with surprising annoyance.

"I promised her I would see to it that her body would be reunited with the earth after she had passed."

"A strange thing for you to promise her, don't you think?" I said to him. "Given the circumstances."

"I can't rest until I know she been laid to rest," he continued.

"Giving people proper funerals isn't exactly something we can accommodate around here lately, you may have noticed."

"Then, why do you wear that crown?" he asked, with what might have been faint sarcasm in his voice.

I said nothing.

~/|\~

I grabbed a shovel from the garage and began to dig in the backyard. I dug a shallow grave in front of a Tesla that had been carried through the air and dropped over the top of the back-yard, its tail end protruding out of the soft soil, peppered with bones and sand and more destruction. The scene here had been so violent, but it faded into the background as I focused on my task. I placed the dressed collections of bones into the wheel-barrow and then wheeled them to the backyard through the side passage by the rusted chain fence. I placed the dead man's dead wife in the grave.

"How deep is this grave?" he asked me, sitting up in the wheelbarrow, watching me place his wife to rest.

"I don't know?" I itched at my beard. "Three feet, four?"

"What kind of person are you?" he said, cackling at the jaw. "Make that six feet, buddy."

I stood there in shock, stunned that I was to bend to the will of a dead man. "Look here, whatever your name is, I don't particularly like being judged by a man who has already met his own judgement. Do you think death is special? Shit, anyone can do it; why should I do what you ask?" It was as if my atti-tude had already changed before he said anything. Out of the fear of getting haunted, I was pleasantly surprised when his answer was humbling.

"What else are you going to do?" he said, having calmed his demeanour. He knew how to adjust his attitude toward me. I picked up the shovel and plunged it into the earth, scraping out three more feet of it. I rested the wife in the deeper hole before I leaned against the shovel protruding from the pile of dirt. We waited there silently for a moment. Perhaps we waited for the other to speak.

"Say something, would ya?" the dead man asked, sounding very panicked. Disoriented, I look around expecting somebody else.

"Me? Why? But…"

"Come on, man! It can't be me. Besides, aren't you the king around here?" he said, indicating my crown. That faint sarcasm again. I thought about it for a moment before I cleared my voice to make a speech.

"Uhh, what's her name?" I asked.

"Marsha."

"Marsha… She was, uh, a fine woman, she loved her husband…"

"Walter," the dead man said, with a hint of shame.

"Walter who also loved her… uh… He made you this promise, and I was happy to assist, you seemed like a pretty cool lady, I hope you kept the bathing suit." I shook my head, feeling ridiculous.

"Thank you," Walter the corpse said. "What am I going to do now?" he cried, as if to plea for God's assistance. "I'm all alone."

"The living not good enough to keep you company? Goddamn it, I'll be around. I sure ain't got nothing to do." I filled in the grave.

That morning the sun didn't rise. Just before dawn, the silence in the air was broken by an explosion that cracked like a thunder strike. Then came a dense cloud of thick, black smoke which eventually turned red so bloody and deep it made my eyes cramp and pulsate. Walter and I remained inside, stationed around the fire as I cooked another can of cat food. He watched me from his rocking chair, fixated on me as I huddled myself together for warmth – the blocking of the sun had forced temperatures to drop well below what I was prepared for.

"Boy, do I wish we could get this thing going," I said as I slapped the TV, the blanket snugged around me. I was getting annoyed by Walter's incessant staring. "What are you looking at?" I finally asked.

"Why do you wear that thing?" he asked me again, pointing to the crown on my head.

"Have you not heard?" I began, "I'm the king of these lands. From the shores of St. John's to the sandy beaches of L.A. there is no other. Therefore, I am master of this realm and keeper of its lands. I decide what lives and what dies in my kingdom."

"Who are you kidding, buddy?" Walter contradicted me. "You're as much of a king as I am Charlie Chaplin… so why do you wear that silly thing?" I decided that arguing with the dead man was futile.

"I took it from a museum. Pretty neat, isn't it? The plaque read that it had belonged to a French royal and some collector got hold of it and put it in the museum. I think it looks—"

"Look at yourself… going around playing make-believe while your body and your sanity suffer…" Walter crossed his arms and shook his head. "You need to be whipped into shape. Time to turn this pathetic sight into a survivalist," he announced.

"And how do you propose we do that?"

"First, we get things in order here. We can't live like this."

I looked around. The particles in the air, metallic-tasting and completely infused with the environment, would be hard to deal with. "I could try to spick'n' things up around here," I mused.

Walter said: "If you clean your place, it will clear up space in your mind."

The activity was itself very relaxing, almost meditative, despite the difficulty of cleaning without running water. The place after a once-over was unrecognizable in the flickering light of the fire. It reflected with the gloss of heavy film from the product I had found underneath the sink. Indistinguishable from a world that lay outside the door. Ash fell from the sky like a sudden heavy snowfall.

"Now we do a little investing," Walter said, nodding his head with approval at the look of the living room.

"What do you mean?" I asked, like a naïve child.

"You're going to have to make a difficult sacrifice." He stared at the last can of cat food and told me what I needed to do. It broke me to do it, but I opened the can and left it out on the kitchen counter as we slept. We woke later to a trading route of cockroaches crawling from the vent in the floor, through the living room, and into the kitchen where they climbed up onto the counter and gathered around the opened can of cat food. I recoiled at the number of large insects trailing one behind one another, a perpetual flow carrying tiny, microscopic balls of tuna and kibble to wherever it was they had come from.

"There you are, a steady supply of food," the corpse said of the cockroaches. "Keep them supplied with a source of food and they will line up for you like a literal buffet."

"That's disgusting… I'm not eating cockroaches," I said, putting my foot down about it.

"Either that or death… and by the looks of you, you're getting to look more like me as time passes. You'll get more protein out of these cockroaches than you will with that cat food, believe me."

I looked at Walter as if I were expecting to read my own face in his skull. I took a fork and stuck it in the back of one of the cockroaches crawling soldier-like in line. I slid it off into the frying pan that sat over top of the fire. The squeaks and squeals the roach made when it hit the heat made me feel for the little guy, but after I had tried it, the cries of pain hardly bothered me after the first couple of batches. The piles began to grow as the fried roach supply ran far beyond what the demand required with still a steady stream going to and from the cat food. There must be millions, I thought to myself as I looked at the vent they appeared from. I laid back, laughing as I made a glutton of myself, feasting upon the fried roaches, seasoned with expired chilli powder, salt, and pepper. It resembled the taste of potato chips, almost exactly like them. Nostalgia came flooding back to me as I had begun to tear up.

"What's wrong?" Walter asked me, as my tears were no easy thing to hide.

"I've forgotten what it's like to feel this stuffed," I babbled, my mouth full of roach paste.

"Take it easy, buddy. You scratched my back and now I'm scratching yours...call it tough love if you want."

"I wasn't sure how long I was going to last out there. I'm in debt to you," I told him, right as I threw up my entire share of roaches into the fire.

Over time, as my stomach adjusted to the new diet, I began to gain some weight and shape in my features. I became strong again despite the deformities the mild levels of radiation had effected on me. Under the close inspection of my scalp, after I had lost all my hair, I discovered that the crown had sat on my head for so long it had merged itself with my scalp. I tried several times to remove it but when I went to do so the skin tugged with it. Veins began to tunnel their way up. My fingernails and toenails came off gradually, one after the other. My front teeth had also slowly fallen out, except for my molars, which after countless days of eating cockroaches became weary of chewing them. Just the thought of eating a single cockroach made me nauseous but they were the only meal in town.

I brought home more canned foods in a brown sack in one of my expeditions around the neighbourhood. I navigated my way through the ghost town, rummaging amongst kitchens and storage closets to supply the army of cockroaches and grow their numbers. When I returned home, I placed the collected cans and mason jars in our kitchen cupboards and filled each shelf from top to bottom. I left a couple for myself in the sack where I went over to the fire across from Walter, who sat in his rocking chair. I pulled out a can opener and peeled the tin seal open and chugged the fruit contents, almost choking on it. Walter was displeased.

"What are you doing!" he shouted. "There's only so many of those left. How long do you think you can make all that in there last?"

"I don't care, I'm sick of these roaches…I need real food. I can't be eating bugs all day."

"How dare you act so ungratefully toward the sacrifice that's kept you alive, and with such improvement too," he said angrily.

"It is indeed a terrible sacrifice, so I think it's best if I immediately stop devouring their population."

"What's a little population control? You keep them from taking us over. It's a necessity that you keep eating them."

"Then I will just stop feeding them."

"But then you would starve."

"Well, then it would seem that we are between a rock and a hard place, old sport," I told Walter as I shook my head to clear the confusion. My speech slurred and half my body dipped down like I was losing the ability to hold myself up. Rock and sulphur pelted the windows, peppered holes through the glass as the violent winds fueled the fires burning the hills. I continued to drink down what was left in the can, forcing my hand in to reach for the fruit that had been stuck at the bottom in thick clumps.

During one of the darkest nights we spent together, Walter finally confessed to the cockroaches' plans. I couldn't tell if I had gone blind, but the thickest smog rolled into the street and completely drenched the place in shadow. Walter told me of their immense intelligence, how they possessed the ability to communicate through telepathy or some kind of interdimensional language only he, the living dead, could decipher. Something along those lines. That night I wondered why, if such an intelligent species existed, why would they intentionally rid themselves of a good chunk of their population to me, the disintegrating memory of a man. Sleep had not come. The hustling of tiny legs coalesced into a collective sound that gave the house a semblance of breath. I could not see them as I laid upon the mattress under the covers, while they blanketed most if not all the surface area of the house. A few steps outside of the bedroom would amount to the crushing of hundreds of them, which I would have to scrape off my feet whenever they touched the floor.

It was around this point that I would find myself snapping at Walter as he tried to make conversation. What had once been an antidote for my boredom became an outlet for my suffering. Headaches, pains, and other ailments were all I could focus on. The place I had come to call home had become far too crowded for a king such as I. By the time the darkness had passed, and the sun had made the bare minimum of visibility possible, I had packed up my things and gathered them to the front door where Walter, just off in the living room rocked in his chair, watching, the sorrowful crack in his voice as he tried talking me out of leaving.

"Where will you go? What will you do? You won't survive out there," he kept reminding me.

"I've made it only so far without you," I said. "You've done so much for me… made me stronger, a little wiser…but I fear for my sanity if I don't leave."

"Who is to say what is sane or insane anymore?" he said. "These words hardly have meaning outside of the world that invented them… a world that has long vanished… What is it you think you will find out there that isn't already here? If you expect to find purpose in the wasteland, I assure you won't find it. Survival is the only commodity that you can afford to hang on to."

"I can't stand it here any longer. I'm so goddamn bored. Anything beats hanging around here rotting away with a corpse and all these roaches. There's still so much I want to see."

"What if I said you could see all you want without ever leaving the comfort of the wonderful home we have created here?"

"I would say that you're a lot crazier than I would have expected from a dead man." A statement I would come to later regret, but after a conversation that went deep, all the while remaining mysteriously vague, I decided to remain until his surprise could be revealed.

In the basement of the house, I uncovered a chest full of old toys. I pulled out a train set that had been carelessly tossed in the trunk amongst the rest of the dolls, G.I. Joes, and Lego pieces. It took me some time to gather all the tracks and loco-motive carts where I assembled them in a circle in the middle of the room. By the time I had set it up, only then had I real-ized the steam engine replica needed a new pair of batteries as the corrosion frosted out of the bottom. My hands trembled and my head boiled at the frustration my attempts at entertain-ing myself had led to. I pulled apart the entire set in my rage and threw pieces all over, breaking several cars and tracks against the cement wall, the plastic exploding into harmful lit-tle shards that posed danger to bare feet in the dark. As I calmed myself and climbed out of the basement, the calluses on my feet took with them several of these broken bits, driving them fur-ther into the skin with each step up the stairs.

I woke to a tender feather touch upon my heels. Thrashing about my bed with irritation, I tossed the covers off to discover that the cockroaches in groups of three on each foot pulled the pieces of plastic from my skin. The roaches crawled off with them to the basement. Before I was able to scratch my head at the strange behaviour, the house lit up with life, strobing and humming with energy. The refrigerator flicked on. Several light bulbs exploded as the surge of electricity forced them from their big sleep. The digital clock on the stove flickered zeroes. The hot water tank below the floor fizzed and moaned. The house trembled as energy flooded throughout its rooms and hallways. I sprung up and out of my bed, dumbfounded by the unfeasi-ble display of sorcery that had taken possession of the place… or perhaps it was my mind. I pinched myself and slapped my face twice to wake myself from this obvious dream. Wake, I did not. All around me was evidence that we finally had power. I rushed to Walter, who sat there with that same annoying skull grin of his. I crossed my arms, trying not to completely give away my amazement.

"What is the meaning of all this?" I asked, looking around the place the electricity had illuminated.

"It's like I said before," Walter said. "What's the sense of leaving your home to a world that has already lost itself? All we have to do is pull back the curtains and take a look." The TV switched on. Static scrolled across the tube and white noise fuzzed out of the speakers. "Go ahead," he said. "Let's see what's on."

In the kitchen, with a whole new set of appliances at my disposal, I whipped up an entirely new recipe to cook the cockroaches, one that had become my specialty and impossible to get sick of. I filled up a large bowl with the insects and began to microwave them. Their bodies discharged their innards that souped into the spices at the centre. I returned to the living room where Walter sat watching cartoons on the loveseat I had positioned in front of the television set. I sat down beside him, snapping my contorted neck into place as the weight of the crown fought back against its natural shape. I looked over at my dead friend, slouched to the side as a cockroach made its exit from his eye socket.

"Did you say something?" I asked him as he stared off blankly, without ever having said a word. "Never mind." I devoured my meal, fixated on the glow of the screen as the roaches went about their business. The train set had been repaired by the cockroaches, and they got much use out of it as they continued their supply chain from the food storage to the vent, down to where their subterranean mechanized civilization had only just begun to grow. The cool electric glow from the television set beamed out into the street by the bay window, all but one of the houses doused in absolute darkness.

Layne Coleman of Toronto had his first non-fiction story, *Oasis of Hope*, published in *Walrus* magazine – it was then nominated for a National Magazine award. *Oasis of Hope* was adapted for the stage and called *Tijuana Cure* – nominated for a Best New play Dora. He was co-writer and co-director of the feature film *The Shape Of Rex*. "Tony Nappo Ruined My Life" is Layne's first fiction story.   *photo by Linda Griffiths*

Beth Goobie is the author of 26 books across genres that include poetry, short fiction, drama, Young Adult, and novels – among them *Before Wings* (CLA Award, Saskatchewan YA Book Award), *The Lottery, The Pain Eater* (Snow Willow Award, Saskatchewan YA Book Award), and *The First Principles of Dreaming*. In 2020, she tied for second in *Tonight It's Poetry*'s annual Saskatoon spoken word championship, which coincided with the acceptance of her fourth poetry collection, *Lookin' For Joy* (2022, with Exile Editions). She lives in Saskatoon.

Andrea Bishop of Vancouver has been published or is forthcoming in *Grain, Orca Literary, The Fiddlehead,* and elsewhere. She was grateful to have participated in a Tin House Winter Workshop and to have had a story nominated by the publisher for the PEN America Robert J. Dau Short Story Prize for Emerging Writers, both in 2021.

@_AndreaBishop, andreabishop.ca   *photo by Belle Ancell*

James MacSwain received a B.A. in English from Mount Allison University, and he studied theatre arts at the University of Alberta. In 1973 he settled in Halifax where he began a career in theatre and arts administration. Since 1980 he has been working in film and

video. MacSwain was the recipient of the 2011 Portia White Prize.   *photo by Tori Fleming*

Kate Cayley has published two short story collections and two collections of poetry. She has won the Trillium Book Award, an O. Henry Prize, the Mitchell Prize for Poetry, and a Chalmers Fellowship, and been a finalist for the Governor General's Award for Fiction, the ReLit Award, and the K. M. Hunter Award. She has also written a number of plays, which have been performed in Canada, the U.S. and the UK. She lives in Toronto with her wife and their three children.

Joe Bongiorno of Montreal is a journalist at the CBC, and a writer of prose who won *Event*'s 2019 Speculative Writing Contest. His short fiction has appeared in *Canadian Notes & Queries, Geist, Maisonneuve,* and *EXILE Quarterly*. He is currently working on a novel and a short story collection. *photo by Anne Guay*

Jennifer DeLeskie is an emerging writer based in Tiohtià:ke (Montreal). Her work has appeared in *The Dalhousie Review,* the anthology *Chronicling the Days: Dispatches from a Pandemic*, and the online publication *QWF Writes!.* Jennifer is a graduate of the Humber  School for Writers Correspondence Program in Creative Writing. She is currently polishing her first novel, a coming-of-age story set in near-future northern Quebec.

Bruce Meyer of Barrie, Ontario, is the author of books of short stories and flash fiction. A new collection of his flash stories, *Sweet Things*, will be published later this year. He recently received "The Editor's Prize" commendation from the Scottish Arts Trust Flash Fiction Award.

photo by Katie Meyer

Rod Carley of North Bay, Ontario, won a Silver Medal from the Independent Publishers Book Awards for his second novel, *Kinmount*; it was also selected as one of 10 books longlisted for the 2021 Leacock Medal for Humour. His first novel, *A Matter of Will*, was a finalist for the Northern Lit Award for Fiction. He has been published in *Cloud Lake Literary, Blank Spaces Magazine, Broadview Magazine,* and the anthology *150 Years Up North and More.* His new short story collection, *Grin Reaping*, is being released in 2022. Rod is an alumnus of the Humber School for Writers. www.rodcarley.ca. *photo by Ed Regan*

John Hart of Toronto was the winner of the 2019 *Toronto Star Short Story Award.* He was a finalist for *The Malahat Review*'s Open Season Awards in 2019, and was on the shortlist for *The Fiddlehead*'s 2020 Fiction Contest. He earned a Letter of Distinction from Humber School of Writers after completing a draft of his first novel with his mentor, Dianne Warren, in 2020.

photo by Karolina Kuras

Jacob Gilligan of Ottawa has been writing after graduating from the Toronto Film School in 2013. Heavily influenced by his mother and her love of film, his writing evolved through writing classes and a love of literature. He has completed several full-length manuscripts and an abundance of short stories. *photo by Stephanie Branch*

THE FINAL CHAPTER
AND THE END OF
A WONDERFUL DECADE

We at Exile have been around long enough to have learned that happenstance is almost everything. You are about to turn right to go home… but, instead, you turn left, and fall in love and never look back. Such is life, and such is how it pretty much happened that the legendary Gloria Vanderbilt, living in Manhattan, came into the life and lives of Exile and its gang of outriding writers and editors.

Back in 2008 we knew nothing about each other… then, by happenstance – introduced by Christopher Adamson, at the time an emerging Exile writer – we had a word… and then two… and the next thing we knew, Gloria was writing her own short stories for Exile, two of which appeared alongside a presentation of her mysterious Picture Boxes in the 2009 *EXILE Quarterly*, Volume 33, Number 3, and then in her 2011 collection, *The Things We Fear Most,* with Exile Editions.

And so was born the relationship that created the inaugural Carter V. Cooper Short Fiction Awards. From then on, we called out to all (and only) Canadian writers for submissions. In the decade following, thousands of stories came in from writers both emerging and at any point in their careers, with over $125,000 awarded! Also, from among the winners and shortlisted – with respect for the talent that came our way, with a honing of their skills through our mentoring programs – 13 books have been published by Exile Editions because of this friendship (see the books, page 216, onward).

Looking back at those first years, when Gloria came to Toronto for the prize-giving and celebratory weekends, bringing her best friends – the cabaret singer Marti Stevens, and close confidant Nancy Biddle of Mayflower family decendency – we were immersed in the eager intent that she and they exhibited. We had big Saturday supper awards galas with 90 guests at Toronto's Turf Club downtown, and the following day afternoon parties of 50 in the backyard of the "House of Exile" on Dale Avenue.

She and the Girls, as we came to call them, had such a good time in those first years, and they so openly admired Exile, that twice after Gloria got home to New York on the Monday she phoned to say that she was increasing the $5,000 prize money to $10,000, and once more to $15,000.

Then she died, at 95, in 2019. But by her arrangement with Anderson, Carter Vanderbilt Cooper's brother, he carried on support for the prize – until at least ten years were completed, until ten volumes of winners and the shortlisted were published, as was her wish. This is that tenth volume, and so the Carter V. Cooper Prize for Short Fiction is done.

But sadness is not what we feel. No. Where you get a blessing you don't witlessly ask for more. You wonder at what has been had, what has been given. All of us at Exile have to say that the whole moment with Gloria Vanderbilt has been extraordinary. Who could have guessed that such a thing could ever have happened? But it did, and now, as all things must, it has come to an end. The trick with endings (all good writers and wise readers know this), however, is to remember that an ending is great because it offers intimations of a beginning. And so we intend to take a moment, certain that when we decide to go right we will inexplicably turn left and there… there, with all the luck in the world, will be something new: the Morley Callaghan competition and short fiction awards to keep writing alive and rewarded, showing that what will be asked is no more and no less than the risk of renewal.

Over the decade of the competition
Exile Editions worked with
13 winning and shortlisted CVC authors,
and we then published their
exceptional short fiction collections.

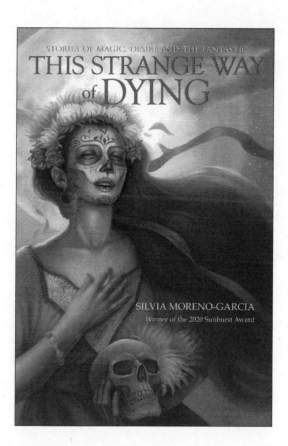

This finalist for an Aurora Award is the exceptional debut collection that spans fantasy, science fiction, horror, and time periods through short stories infused with Mexican folklore yet firmly rooted in a reality that transforms as the fantastic erodes the rational.

"Silvia Moreno-Garcia's stories are sensitive and haunting portraits of worlds where the impossible and the real live side by side. Hers is a rare and wonderful talent." —Lavie Tidhar, World Fantasy Award-winning author of *Osama*

One of Exile's top 10 selling print and ebook titles in 2020 and 2021.

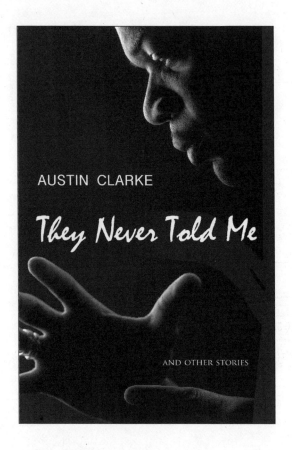

From the winner of the Giller, Commonwealth, Trillium, and Writers' Trust prizes, comes this outstanding collection of eight stories.

"[The book has] a fidelity to the kind of sensual language that has always been a hallmark of the author's writing." —*National Post*

"While many of these stories are stationed in memory of the new immigrant experience, the titular story strikes a harmony of hurt as an elderly Barbadian immigrant stumbles around Toronto in blackface, lost in a fog of nostalgia, his struggle with age resurrecting and reciprocating his struggle with racism. The parallel is just the tip of the iceberg of insight Clarke's wisdom offers in these stories."
—*Telegraph-Journal/Salon Books*

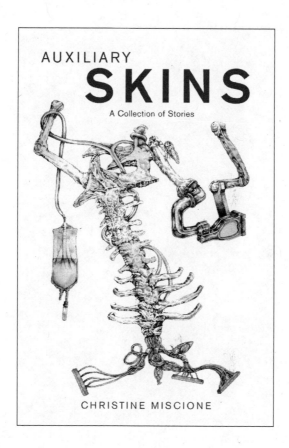

Winner of the ReLit Best Short Fiction Award.

Christine Miscione's remarkable debut collection *Auxiliary Skins* exists somewhere in that chasm between bodily function and souled-ness, illumiinating all that's perilous, beautiful and raw about being human.

"Miscione excels at writing about horrible things in beautiful ways. Her prose is not only deft and neat, but often wrenchingly lovely, so that much of the text comes across like a suppurating wound wrapped in hand-stitched lace."

—*Quill & Quire*

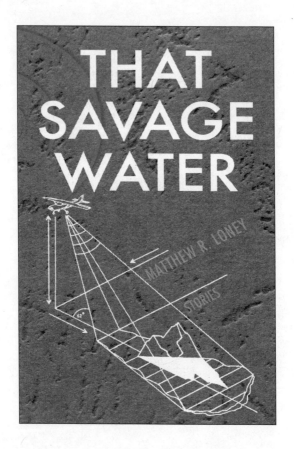

That Savage Water is a striking collection of stories about travels abroad, told in language that is rich in description, full of lucid and lively textures, smells and sensations that transports the reader to places not on the average itinerary. From familiar departure lounges on to foreign cities steeped in history, the enticing turquoise beaches of picture-perfect postcards, the desolate mountain ranges that take one well off the beaten track, bathing in the sacred Ganges, and fringe indulgences in Cambodian brothels – and a return to a northern Canadian cabin where the father of a tsunami victim contemplates how a surge of savage water forever changed the lives of so many, most poignantly, his own.

"Matthew Loney's prose is gorgeous and filled with wonderful descriptions that allow us to feel what the characters do... It is amazing that this is the author's fiction debut. The term 'abroad' gets a whole new meaning here."

—*Books, Movies, and Judaica*

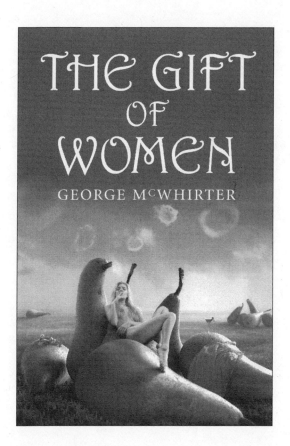

Finalist for the ReLit Best Short Fiction Award.

George McWhirter grounds his delightful characters in the real, while his sharp wit and creative scenarios border on the fantastical: a woman adopts a dolphin-man; an Irish madam runs a railroad bordello in the desert; a devoted husband drives his childless, belly-dancing wife to Greek *tavernas* with the ambition to quicken their lagging fertility; a Kurdish barber has a cure for hair loss, but not the loss of his wife and family in Iraq; a Mexican *campesino* swears his machete-severed ear is a seashell tuned to the Pacific Ocean. *The Gift of Women* is about religion and sexuality, the surreal and the magical, a tale-telling of earthy and remarkable women.

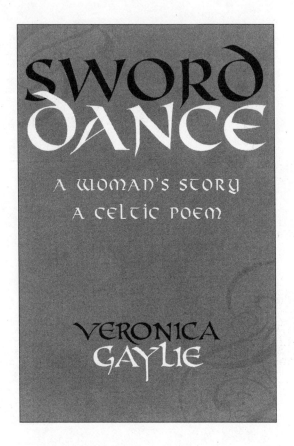

A woman's childhood life in Scotland and a new life in Canada are explored by her daughter in this memoir-style prose-poetry that profoundly embodies the classic Canadian immigrant tale.

The characters, beginning with the emigrating ancestors Tom, Dick, and Harry, to the everyday Glasgow cousin, John Lennon in a scheme to raise pigs, and a bicycle riding Richard Nixon who arrives just after a factory blow-up, to the author's father, a young soldier who catches the eye of his wife-to-be at the glove counter in Woolworth's, are all real.

Framed by a prologue and epilogue – with an introduction by the author, and a "A Short Glaswegian Guide" (Glossary) on end – the story is told in a working-class vernacular, the voices gritty, witty and distinct as they produce a beautiful tapestry by way of the music and language of Glaswegian storytelling.

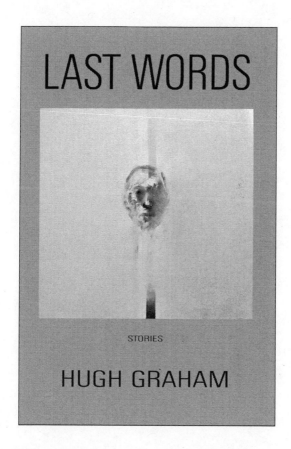

LAST WORDS

STORIES

HUGH GRAHAM

Finalist for the Danuta Gleed Best First Book of Short Stories Award.

Hugh Graham captures the passage of years, the progression of accumulation and recurrence, the present as dammed up history. Without warning, a world on the road to epiphany. And that world, threatened with disaster. Figures emerge, often from twilight. Children who do not fear death, travellers doomed to inertia, concupiscent women, bloody-minded intellectuals, haunted drunks, decaying diplomats, and Death as the man in the attic room. In the end, the gaze of a child become a man. Eleven stories of clarity and dark empathy.

"In the linked short-fiction collection *Last Words*, Hugh Graham has his way with a foundational conceit of western literature and tries to squeeze a bit more juice out of it." —*Quill & Quire*

As the quiet, awkward Madeleine finds herself amid a tumultuous mix of pluralism, soul-searching matters of family breakdown, personal fragility, and human connection, she discovers that love is neither Muslim nor Christian nor secular

This is a tale for our times, enveloping the reader in a fictionalized travel memoir that blossoms with vivid language and imagery accessible to all. The storyteller's family were refugees, and her experiences following their assimilation into Canadian society mirrors many of the personal confrontations, sacrifices, and moments of discovery that underlie family dynamics with each new wave of émigrés.

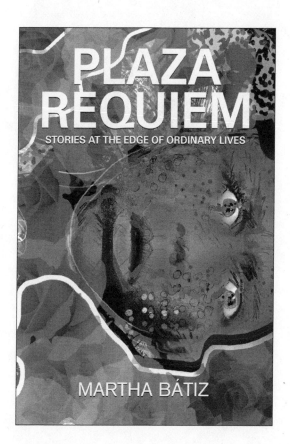

Winner, Best Popular Fiction, Latino Book Awards.

These stories shimmer with the vindication that women attain, in their qualities to survive against all odds, a certain new-found power after their darkest moments.

As an emerging writer Bátiz is, with precision and haunting vision, reminiscent of Joyce Carol Oates, Shirley Jackson, and the Cuban author Leonardo Padura.

"A theme drawing *Plaza Requiem* together [is] the notion of "the disappeared"…a euphamism for the victims of state terrorism… But Bátiz also explores disappearance in a larger, metaphorical sense, especially as forms of violence against women. … In Bátiz's telling, disappearance as repression, while not ordinary, is too common." —*The Globe and Mail*

"Martha Bátiz knows what it takes to find your voice in a new country."
—Shelagh Rogers, CBC's *The Next Chapter*

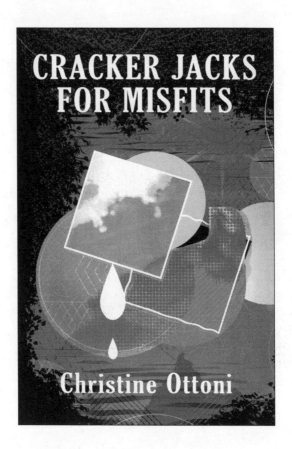

Finalist for the Bressani Best First Book Award.

Christine Ottoni has crafted a finely layered narrative of interconnected short stories about discovering independence, strength, and the power to love in which Naomi, Joanne, Jake, and Marce find themselves caught in the crosshairs of modern-day chaos marked by urban claustrophobia and loneliness. *Cracker Jacks for Misfits* is a contemporary and poignant portrait of the moment when childhood becomes a new country of adult commitments...

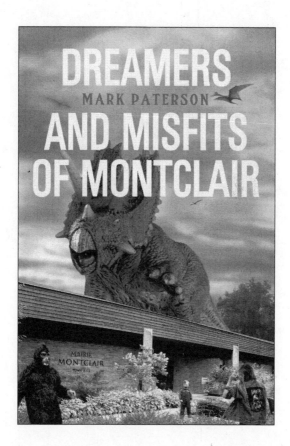

Mark Paterson introduces the town of Montclair, a fictional suburb of Montreal, to celebrate characters through wise and humorous stories that explore people's extraordinary lives in suburbia's little wild spaces.

"Paterson's writing shines throughout *Dreamers and Misfits of Montclair*. His language is concrete, poetic, and radiant." —*Literary Review of Canada*

"[Paterson is] punchy, off-kilter, and highly imaginative." —*Quill & Quire*

"Compellingly narrated with a slacker's eye for the bizarre, the writing seems effortless." —*The Globe and Mail*

"Mark Paterson is a great storyteller." —*Montreal Review of Books*

"Mark Paterson is a funny, often empathetic writer." —*The Malahat Review*

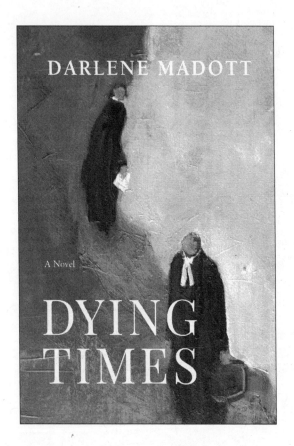

Dying Times is the story of a successful though conflicted lady litigator, told with a dark undercurrent of humour that underpins this striking meditation on dying, and discovering a meaningful approach to living.

"There comes a point in people's lives, when they reach a certain age, when everyone around them starts to die… Madott helps us get to know…about dealing with death while also understanding how to live." —*Toronto Star*

"[The narrator] is snared in a spiderweb of rivalry, resentment and grief in this wise and compelling meditation on death, loss and forgiveness. Written in a frank and crisp style, *Dying Times* offers compelling life lessons for the young as well as the aged. I couldn't put it down."

—Sandra Martin, contributing writer for *The Globe and Mail*

EQUIPOISE

ten stories

KATIE ZDYBEL

The women of *Equipoise* find their positionality in life in relation to the women around them as they maintain a balance within the tension of their opposing female roles, landscapes, friendships, rivalries, victories, and catastrophes.

Equipoise was shortlisted for the HarperCollins/UBC Prize for Best New Fiction, and was a Finalist for the ReLit Best Short Fiction Award.

"I admire Katie Zdybel's incisive, pared-down prose, her insights into womanhood, family, and friendships." —Joyce Carol Oates

"*Equipoise* begs comparison with Alice Munro… I was deeply altered by the stories and their ties to the cold and bewildering speed, excess and isolation of contemporary life. Katie Zdybel possesses an acutely intelligent feminine gaze that is attuned to the abrasion of the outside world and the possibility of reinvention." —*Malahat Review*

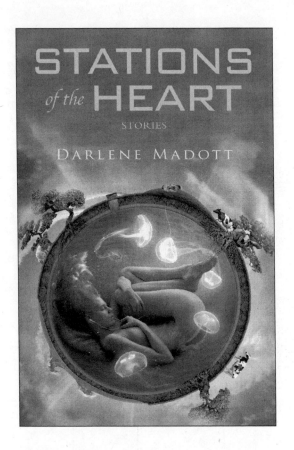

Winner of the Bressani Best Novel Award.

Darlene Madott, as a teller of interconnected love stories – stories about women, and the men who enter and exit their lives – has a way of circling moments of unresolved emotional ambiguity, circling until, with a sudden intensity, she slices directly to the heart of experience. What is remarkable about Madott's women is that they remain open and vulnerable despite betrayal and sorrow: from station to station, they carry their crosses. Each is on a singular pilgrimage, intent on embracing life openly and willingly, seeking something rare in our times – communion with the self through communion with another.

A dynamic short story collection that is wild with laughter, confronting pathos, rage and humour in ways that only Rooke's subversive, edgy, and wildly entertaining writing can approach.

"The 20 pieces that make up *Wide World in Celebration and Sorrow: Acts of Kamikaze Fiction* could be considered a kind of literary tasting menu for those unfamiliar with Rooke's oeuvre... and many of Rooke's signature registers — the absurdist humour, the literary and philosophical allusiveness, the sudden violence are on display [and...] interact with each other as readily as with a reader."

—*National Post*

CVC NINE TO ONE
THE WINNERS AND THE SHORTLISTED

CVC9:

Katie Zdybel – "The Critics"
  (winner, Emerging Writer – Thornbury, Ontario)
Susan Swan – "The Oil Man's Tale"
  (co-winner, Any Career Point Writer – Toronto, Ontario)
Linda Rogers – "Rapunzel"
  (co-winner, Any Career Point Writer – Victoria, British Columbia)

• Shortlisted:
Darlene Madott – "Newton's Law"
  (Toronto, Ontario)
Lue Palmer – "Wata Tika Dan Blood"
  (Toronto, Ontario)
Kate Felix-Segriff – "The Poet of Blind River"
  (Toronto, Ontario)
Marion Quednau – "Sunday Drive to Gun Club Road"
  (Sunshine Coast, British Columbia)
A.S. Penne – "All That Can Be Done"
  (Sechelt, British Columbia)
Christine Ottoni – "Plastic"
  (Hamilton, Ontario)
Sarah Tolmie – "Precor"
  (Waterloo, Ontario)
Katie Zdybel – "Honey Maiden"
  (Thornbury, Ontario)

CVC8:

Leanne Milech – "The Light in the Closet"
  (winner, Emerging Writer – Toronto, Ontario)
Edward Brown – "Remember Me"
  (co-winner, Any Career Point Writer – Toronto, Ontario)
Priscila Uppal – "Elevator Shoes"
  (co-winner, Any Career Point Writer – Toronto, Ontario)

• Shortlisted:
Cara Marks – "Aurora Borealis"
  (Victoria, British Columbia)
William John Wither – "The Bulbous It with No Eyelids"
  (London, Ontario)
Mark Paterson – "My Uncle, My Barbecue Chicken Deliveryman"
  (Lorraine, Quebec)
Lorna Crozier – "Rebooting Eden"
  (Vancouver Island, British Columbia)
Bruce Meyer – "Cantique de Jean Racine"
  (Barrie, Ontario)
Christine Miscione – "Your Failing Heart."
  (Hamilton, Ontario)
Martha Bátiz – "Suspended"
  (Richmond Hill, Ontario)
Andrea Bradley – "No One Is Watching"
  (Oakville, Ontario)

CVC7:

Halli Villegas – "Road Kill"
  (winner, Emerging Writer – Mount Forest, Ontario)
Seán Virgo – "Sweetie"
  (winner, Any Career Point Writer – Eastend, Saskatchewan)

• Shortlisted:
Iryn Tushabe – "A Separation"
  (Saskatoon, Saskatchewan)
Katherine Fawcett – "The Pull of Old Rat Creek"
  (Squamish, British Columbia)
Darlene Madott – "Winners and Losers"
  (Toronto, Ontario)
Jane Callen – "Grace"
  (Victoria, British Columbia)
Yakos Spiliotopoulos – "Grave Digger"
  (Toronto, Ontario)
Chris Urquhart – "Skinbound"
  (Toronto, Ontario)
Norman Snider – "Husband Material"
  (Toronto, Ontario)
Carly Vandergriendt – "Resurfacing"
  (Montreal, Quebec)
Linda Rogers – "Breaking the Sound Barrier"
  (Victoria, British Columbia)

CVC6:

Matthew Heiti – "For They Were Only Windmills"
  (winner, Emerging; Sudbury, Ontario)
Helen Marshall – "The Gold Leaf Executions"
  (winner, Any Career Point; Sarnia, Ontario)

• Shortlisted:
Diana Svennes-Smith – "Stranger in Me"
  (Eastend, Saskatchewan)
Sang Kim – "Kimchi"
  (Toronto, Ontario)
A.L. Bishop – "Hospitality"
  (Niagara Falls, Ontario)
Katherine Govier – "Elegy: Vixen, Swan, Emu"
  (Toronto, Ontario)
Sheila McClarty – "The Diamond Special"
  (Oakbank, Manitoba)
Caitlin Galway – "Bonavere Howl"
  (Toronto, Ontario)
Bruce Meyer – "The Slithy Toves"
  (Barrie, Ontario)
Frank Westcott – "It Was a Dark Day – Not a Stormy Night –
  In Tuck-Tea-Tee-Uck-Tuck"
  (Alliston, Ontario)
Martha Bátiz – "Paternity, Revisited"
  (Richmond Hill, Ontario)
Leon Rooke – "Open the Door"
  (Toronto, Ontario)
Norman Snider – "How Do You Like Me Now?"
  (Toronto, Ontario)

CVC5:

Lisa Foad – "How to Feel Good"
    (winner, Emerging; Toronto, Ontario)
Nicholas Ruddock – "Mario Vargas Llosa"
    (winner, Any Career Point; Guelph, Ontario)

• Shortlisted:
Hugh Graham – "After Me"
    (Toronto, Ontario)
Josip Novakovich – "Dunavski Pirat"
    (Montreal, Quebec)
Leon Rooke – "Sara Mago et al"
    (Toronto, Ontario)
Jane Eaton Hamilton – "The Night SS Sloan Undid His Shirt"
    (Vancouver, British Columbia)
Bruce Meyer – "Tilting"
    (Barrie, Ontario)
Priscila Uppal – "Bed Rail Entrapment Risk Notification Guide"
    (Toronto, Ontario)
Christine Miscione – "Spring"
    (Hamilton, Ontario)
Veronica Gaylie – "Tom, Dick, and Harry"
    (Vancouver, British Columbia)
Maggie Dwyer – "Chihuahua"
    (Commanda, Ontario)
Bart Campbell – "Slim and the Hangman"
    (Vancouver, British Columbia)
Linda Rogers – "Raging Breath and Furious Mothers"
    (Victoria, British Columbia)
Lisa Pike – "Stellas"
    (Windsor, Ontario)

CVC4:

Jason Timermanis – "Appetite"
    (winner, Emerging; Toronto, Ontario)
Hugh Graham – "The Man"
    (winner, Any Career Point; Toronto, Ontario)

• Shortlisted:
Helen Marshall – "The Zhanell Adler Brass Spyglass"
    (Sarnia, Ontario)
K'ari Fisher – "Saddle Up!"
    (Burns Lake, British Columbia)
Linda Rogers – "Three Strikes"
    (Victoria, British Columbia)
Susan P. Redmayne – "Baptized"
    (Oakville, Ontario)
Matthew R. Loney – "The Pigeons of Peshawar"
    (Toronto, Ontario)
Erin Soros – "Morning is Vertical"
    (Vancouver, British Columbia)
Gregory Betts – "Planck"
    (St. Catharines, Ontario)
George McWhirter – "Sisters in Spades"
    (Vancouver, British Columbia)
Madeline Sonik – "Punctures"
    (Victoria, British Columbia)
Leon Rooke – "Slain By a Madam"
    (Toronto, Ontario)

CVC3:

Sang Kim – "When John Lennon Died"
    (winner, Emerging; Toronto, Ontario)
Priscila Uppal – "Cover Before Striking"
    (co-winner, Any Career Point; Toronto, Ontario)
Austin Clarke – "They Never Told Me"
    (co-winner, Any Career Point; Toronto, Ontario)

• Shortlisted:
George McWhirter – "Tennis"
    (Vancouver, British Columbia)
David Somers – "Punchy Sells Out"
    (Winnipeg, Manitoba)
Leon Rooke – "Conditional Sphere of Everyday Historical Life"
    (Toronto, Ontario)
Helen Marshall – "Lessons in the Raising of Household Objects"
    (Sarnia, Ontario)
Yakos Spiliotopoulos – "Black Sheep"
    (Toronto, Ontario)
Greg Hollingshead – "Mother / Son"
    (Toronto, Ontario)
Matthew R. Loney – "A Fire in the Clearing"
    (Toronto, Ontario)
Rob Peters – "Sam's House"
    (Vancouver, British Columbia)
Liz Windhorst Harmer – "Teaching Strategies"
    (Hamilton, Ontario)

CVC2:

Christine Miscione – "Skin, Just"
   (winner, Emerging; Hamilton, Ontario)
Leon Rooke – "Here Comes Henrietta Armani"
   (co-winner, Any Career Point; Toronto, Ontario)
Seán Virgo – "Gramarye"
   (co-winner, Any Career Point; East End, Saskatchewan)

• Shortlisted:
Kelly Watt – "The Things My Dead Mother Says"
   (Flamborough, Ontario)
Darlene Madott – "Waiting (An Almost Love Story)"
   (Toronto, Ontario)
Linda Rogers – "Darling Boy"
   (Victoria, British Columbia)
Daniel Perry – "Mercy"
   (Toronto, Ontario)
Amy Stuart – "The Roundness"
   (Toronto, Ontario)
Phil Della – "I Did It for You"
   (Vancouver, British Columbia)
Jacqueline Windh – "The Night the Floor Jumped"
   (Vancouver, British Columbia)
Kris Bertin – "Tom Stone and Co."
   (Halifax, Nova Scotia)
Martha Bátiz – "The Last Confession"
   (Richmond Hill, Ontario)

CVC1:

Silvia Moreno-Garcia – "Scales as Pale as Moonlight"
    (co-winner, Emerging; Vancouver, British Columbia)
Frank Westcott – "The Poet"
    (co-winner, Emerging; Shelburne, Ontario)
Ken Stange – "The Heart of a Rat"
    (winner, Any Career Point; Toronto, Ontario)

• Shortlisted:
Hugh Graham – "Through the Sky"
    (Toronto, Ontario)
Leigh Nash – "The Field Trip"
    (Toronto, Ontario)
Rishma Dunlop – "Paris"
    (Toronto, Ontario)
Zoe Stikeman – "Single-Celled Amoeba"
    (Toronto, Ontario)
Kristi-ly Green – "The Patient"
    (Toronto, Ontario)
Gregory Betts – "To Tell You"
    (Oakville, Ontario)
Richard Van Camp – "On the Wings of This Prayer"
    (Edmonton, Alberta)